A TIME FOR ADVENTURE

Gerry MacNeil's Time Travel Saga

Mel RJ Smith

A Time for Adventure
Copyright © 2016 Mel R.J Smith
Published in 2016 by Merijo Prints and Amazon Createspace
Cover Design by © Merijo Prints (Images courtesy of Adobe Stock Images)
Book Formatting by Merijo Prints
ISBN: 9781530896158

All rights reserved. Printed in the United Kingdom. No part of this book may be used or reproduced in any manner whatsoever without written permission, except in the case of brief quotations in critical articles or reviews.

This book is a work of fiction. Names, characters, businesses, organizations, places, events and incidents either are the product of the author's imagination or are used fictitiously. Any resemblance to actual persons, living or dead, events, or locales is entirely coincidental.

A Time for Adventure
Copyright © 2016 Mel R.J Smith
Published in 2016 by Merijo Prints and Amazon Createspace
Cover Design by © Merijo Prints (Images courtesy of Adobe Stock Images)
Book Formatting by Merijo Prints
ISBN: 9781530896158

All rights reserved. Printed in the United Kingdom. No part of this book may be used or reproduced in any manner whatsoever without written permission, except in the case of brief quotations in critical articles or reviews.

This book is a work of fiction. Names, characters, businesses, organizations, places, events and incidents either are the product of the author's imagination or are used fictitiously. Any resemblance to actual persons, living or dead, events, or locales is entirely coincidental.

A TIME FOR ADVENTURE

Gerry MacNeil's Time Travel Saga

Mel RJ Smith

To Jayne
Happy reading
Best regards

I dedicate this book to Rosa Teoli for her belief, for pushing me on and keeping me going.
Thanks Babes.

CHAPTER ONE

Sunday 23rd September, 8.00 am

"I say, I'm so awfully sorry," a female voice said.

Gerry tried to focus on the voice but his vision was blurred as he lay there, stunned.

"Daddy's going to be so angry with me," the voice said.

As Gerry lifted himself onto one elbow, the image behind the voice became gradually clearer. In her mid to late twenties, she was an attractive young lady with serene blue eyes, soft skin and brunette curls that fell beneath her cloche hat. That's the next thing Gerry noticed - her attire. The pale green frock, stocking legs and golf shoes gave her not only an elegant, classy look but also reminded Gerry of a 1920s flapper.

She looked down at him, lying helpless on the damp, late September grass.

"I – I didn't see you," she said. "You seemed to appear from nowhere. I did shout but it was too late."

Gerry winced as he probed the bump that was forming, a reminder of where her ball had hit.

"It's fine," he said. "Can you help me up?" He extended his arm towards her.

"Oh, of course. I'm so sorry, how rude of me," she replied, helping Gerry to his feet. "Daddy is going to be so angry," she said, once again.

"Why?" he asked. "I'm Gerry, by the way."

Gerry stared at her as she replied. She seemed familiar to him but he couldn't place her.

"Eloise. Eloise Ponsonby," she replied. "Daddy doesn't like it when I play. That's why I started early, before any of the gentlemen arrived. The other gentlemen, I mean."

"Oookay," Gerry said, bemused with her concern. "So why are you dressed like that? Is it a fancy dress competition?"

"I beg your pardon?" she replied, looking Gerry up and down. "One might just say the same about you." Disappointed by his comment, she turned her head to one side, then added, "Mr. Bumble Bee."

"Bumble bee?" he said sharply. "I think my knock was a little more than a sting."

"Of course but you do look rather bright," she said with a smile.

Gerry looked down at his own attire and was shocked by what he saw. A two-tone pair of Oxfords, yellow and black argyle socks, checked plus-fours and, to top it off, a yellow and black striped pullover vest. His brand new tailor-made golf clubs had also been replaced and, lying at his feet, there was now a canvas bag containing a set of well-used hickory clubs.

"What the heck?" he said.

The numbers, 3 and 10. He remembered the numbers but that's all and now he was here, not only dressed as a nineteen twenties golfer but it seemed he really was in the 1920s.

Gerry couldn't believe it. He loved this era; the roaring twenties with its flappers and gangsters and the Great Depression with bootlegging and money laundering. He had watched so many films and read book after book on the subject, often dreaming he was born in that era.

"Come on," Eloise said, disturbing his thoughts. "Let's go and sort that bump of yours out."

Gerry picked up the clubs to follow her and, as she headed in the direction of the clubhouse, he felt apprehensive as to what else might occur.

As they approached the building, Gerry recognised it immediately and was surprised how little it had changed, whereas the surrounding landscape had altered substantially. The putting green was gone, to be replaced with a stone staircase that rose up from an ornate fountain. These lead up to what should have been the patio area, where Gerry enjoyed a pint or three after a hard day of golfing. This area was now, or once was, a gravel driveway and was now filled with an assortment of vintage cars that were parked in front of the grand structure itself.

Kelsey Hall golf club was a large three-storey structure, constructed from brick and flint-rock. It had two wings that sat adjacent to the core, which itself boasted six ornate columns leading to the main entrance.

"Welcome to my home," Eloise said, leading Gerry past the columns and through the great oak door.

"Your home?" Gerry questioned. "Don't you mean golf club?"

"I was born here, Bumble. You are such a strange creature," she replied. "Surely you know Daddy only invites his most influential friends to play here. You won't tell him what happened, promise you won't."

"My lips are sealed," he said.

"Oh, Bumble, you are a dear." She kissed Gerry on the cheek and he hadn't noticed it before but her aroma gave him a sense of déjà vu. The smell and warmth of cigar tobacco infused with lush flowers filled his nasal senses, reminding Gerry of sunshine and good times.

"Your perfume. What is it?" he asked. "I've smelt it before."

"It's Molinard Habantia. Daddy brought it back from one of his trips abroad."

"Havana, to be precise, my darling."

"Daddy, you're up! Let me introduce Bumble. I mean, Gerry."

The man before them stood tall with certitude and was dressed in an ivory Brooks Brothers suit, blue silk pocket square and a highly-polished pair of brown and white wingtips, so it was immediately obvious to Gerry that Eloise's Daddy was a man of wealth and distinction. Eloise was certainly her father's daughter; the resemblance was uncanny, especially his same blue eyes, high cheek bones and prominent chin.

He took hold of Gerry's hand with a firm grip and shook it vigorously.

"We've met before," he said.

"You have?" Eloise asked.

Have we, Gerry thought.

"MacNeil, if I'm not mistaken. PD introduced us, briefly."

PD, Gerry thought. There's only one PD he knew and that was his boss, Peter Dann, but surely not.

"Peter, Mr. Ponsonby?" Gerry questioned, "The rotund yorkshireman?"

"That's the fellow but please call me Georgie," he replied. "Now, tell me how you two came to meet?"

"I was ummmm, gol......," Eloise started to say, causing Gerry to interrupt.

"Your daughter came to my rescue, sir."

"Oh, pray tell."

"I was searching for my lost ball amongst the trees," he lied. "Something startled me and, getting up too quickly, I clumsily knocked my head on a low branch. Eloise was passing and invited me back to dress the wound."

"Is that right?" he said, raising his eyebrows at his daughter.

Eloise looked down at her feet, trying in vain to hide her lie.

"Yes, Daddy," she said, "that's what happened."

Georgie could read his daughter like a book but he let it go.

"Very well," he said. "Now I must dash, as I have an important meeting to attend."

With that, Georgie brushed past them. Pausing briefly, he laid his hand on Gerry's shoulder. "Nice story, Bumble," he whispered, "and nice to meet you again, MacNeil. I'm sure my daughter will take good care of you," he said, before disappearing out the door. "Oh, and Eloise. Next time, put your clubs away," he added.

* * *

Gerry sat at the large Victorian table, which was easily able to seat ten staff, the pine now worn after years of service. Laying his hand on the wood, he felt its texture and imagined the many lavish meals that would have been prepared over the years, the smell of freshly-baked bread fuelling his imagination. He gazed around the warm kitchen, taking in its features, many of which still remained Victorian in style.

Across the table and set back in a recess, stood a blackened cast-iron range. Still hot from the baking, the rising heat gently stirred the copper cooking utensils that hung on chain and hook from the high ceiling. To its left, set against the wall, stood a dresser, every shelf filled with an assortment of pots and pans that had seen many a year of hard labour.

The scullery was next, which may have once been lit by a solitary candle but was now ablaze with light from an overhead lamp, illuminating a figure that was bent over the sink. Running the cold water over a cloth, in the hope it would help, Eloise felt guilty for what had happened earlier, though she was certain no-one was there when the ball struck.

"I won't keep you a moment, Bumble," she told him.

"It's fine. Take your time. I'm just admiring your house. Has it been in your family long?"

"Yes. My grandfather, Sir George Ponsonby, acquired it in the mid 1800s."

"I bet it could tell a tale or two," he said. "What the butler saw and all that."

Eloise laughed.

"Old Archie? He wouldn't see much at all, bless him. He's been in Daddy's employ since long before I was born."

"No, I mean….," Gerry started to say but thought better of it. He didn't want to have to explain the images of twentieth century postcards to the lady of the house.

Eloise placed the damp cloth on Gerry's head, the coolness easing the bump almost immediately.

"Now just hold that there, while I arrange some refreshments," she said, before disappearing from the kitchen, leaving Gerry alone. Or so he thought.

"Hello, little fella," he said, to a mouse that caught his attention as it scurried across the kitchen floor. The mouse stopped dead in its tracks and looked up at Gerry, as if listening to him.

"What is all this?" Gerry asked the mouse. "Do you know why I am here? Why? Why am I here, my little friend?"

Before the mouse, who in fact reminded Gerry of his neighbour, Sid, moved on, a bell started to chime. The mouse looked from Gerry to the bell, before continuing on its journey. Gerry watched with interest, as it squeezed behind the dresser, stopping briefly to give him one last glance.

Gerry hadn't noticed the servant bells when he was surveying the room. They were in a row of five and fixed to the wall just above the dumb waiter, each labelled with brass plaques, indicating their source. The one labelled 'Front Door' chimed once again.

"Who were you talking to?" Eloise asked, when she returned. She handed Gerry a bottle of ginger beer.

"Thanks, just what the doctor ordered," he said. "Oh, I was just muttering to myself."

"Maybe that bump is worse than it looks," she jokingly replied, before removing the cloth and studying the injury.

"Looks like you have eager visitors," Gerry said, pointing to the bell that now had an impatient ring to it.

"That's okay. Archie will answer it."

"You sure he'll be able to see who it is?" Gerry asked.

"Oh Bumble, you are a card. Come on then. Let's go find out for ourselves, shall we?"

Barely managing to take a gulp of the ginger beer, he placed the bottle awkwardly on the table, before being pulled with a rush from the kitchen, up a spiral stairwell and back into the entrance hall.

Eloise still holding his hand which, in truth, Gerry liked, they almost came to an abrupt halt. Well, they would have done, had Gerry not been shoeless. Having removed his Oxfords earlier, he started to slide. The freshly-polished dark oak floorboards held no grip or friction on his stocking feet and he careered past Eloise, who had no choice but to release her grip and watch, as Gerry slid on towards the door and the unsuspecting butler.

"Archie! Look out!" Eloise hollered but, practically blind, and obviously deaf too, as well as unaware of what was happening behind him, Archie continued to dutifully open the door.

Gerry, now trying his best to stay upright, sped on towards the gaping hole and crashed full force into the surprised visitor. They both toppled backwards, landing in a heap on the dusty ground.

"Bumble, are you okay?" Eloise asked, as she helped Gerry to his feet for the second time that day. "David, nice of you to drop in," she added.

Getting to his feet, David dusted himself down, before eyeing Gerry with a disdainful look.

"Literally, wouldn't you say?" he replied.

Gerry took an instant dislike to this tall, well-built, blonde-haired, man but put his hand out to shake nonetheless.

"Sorry," he said, "I couldn't stop in time. It's the floor. It's a bit slippery."

David reluctantly offered his own hand in return.

"That's how it's supposed to be in a well-run household, isn't it?" he said. "That's what staff are paid to do."

Gerry couldn't be sure but he could have sworn David added 'Dummkoff' under his breath. Never trust a man with a weak grip, or eyes that are too close together, Gerry's father had once told him. David had both and Gerry knew from that moment that this man was definitely not to be trusted.

David was the first to lead the way back into the house, completely ignoring Archie as he did so. Eloise held back, grabbing Gerry by the arm.

"I'm sorry," she said. "About David, I mean. His manners are not one of his best qualities."

"Does he have any?" Gerry replied.

Eloise let out a giggle.

"Who is he, anyway?" Gerry asked.

"David Steinberg. He's Daddy's business partner. He's more than likely here to see him."

Gerry nodded at Archie, as they both followed David back inside. He had the same feeling about the butler as he did earlier about Eloise. He seemed familiar but he couldn't place him. Gerry looked back over his shoulder for a second glimpse. As Archie was heading out the door, he smiled, gave Gerry a sneaky wink and closed the door behind him.

*　*　*

To help with the guilt of two accidents in the same morning, Eloise invited Gerry to stay for dinner and for the night. She instructed that the guest bedroom and a pair of shoes be made ready. Gerry accepted the offer for two reasons: one, he wanted to get to know Eloise better and, two, where else was he going to go? His house probably wouldn't have been built yet.

CHAPTER TWO

Sunday 23rd September, 11:30 am

The two of them sat opposite each other, in a quiet corner of the Just Inn Time public house and what they had to say was for their ears only.

"Good choice of name for a place to meet but what's so important?"

"He's here."

"Good. At last. Where?"

"Back at Kelsey Hall. He arrived this morning."

"Is he safe?"

"I would say he's in good hands, yes."

"Eloise?"

"Yes, Eloise."

"Good….. That's very good."

"I best get back."

"Okay. Keep me informed and keep him safe."

A TIME FOR ADVENTURE

"Don't worry. No harm will come to him. It was meant to be."

Peter picked up the tankard and savoured the hops, as he watched his partner leave. "Well, Mr. MacNeil, my dear fellow, you're here at last," he said to himself.

* * *

The bedroom was large and smelled of fresh linen. A bay window was at one end, with the curtains drawn back to allow the natural light to filter in and fill the room. Gerry sat on the window ledge and looked out over the estate. This time he was alone and could think clearly about the day's events.

Everything happens for a reason; he knew that from past experiences. He also felt that he was here for a reason but what was it? That was the burning question. Why the similarities with the people from his future time? It was also clear that Georgie had met him before but when? Surely he would know if they had. There were so many unanswered questions.

As he sat there contemplating, a lone figure walked across the courtyard below. Eloise.

Gerry released the window catch and lifted the window above his head, holding it in place, just in case he received another bump on his head.

"Hi," he said.

"Oh, Bumble," she replied, looking up at him. "How's your room? I know it isn't much."

"It's fine, just dandy," he said. "Where are you off to?"

"I'm about to take Bouncer for a walk. Would you care to join us?"

"I'll be right down," he said.

Gerry secured the window and stood watching for a moment as Eloise played, teasing the German Shepherd with a stick, before throwing it for him to fetch.

Could she be the reason? He hoped she was.

* * *

"Tell me about yourself, Gerry," she said. "Why are you here?"

Gerry thought for a moment as they walked arm in arm, following Bouncer as he ran on ahead.

"To save the world, rescue the girl, fall in love," he replied.

She laughed.

"No. Really. Why? Are you here to help Daddy with his new business?"

Bouncer returned, jumping up to show his affection.

"I'm a time traveller," Gerry replied. "I came here from the future to save you from a ferocious beast of a dog."

"Bumble, you're such a tease."

They walked for a good two hours, covering most of the grounds. Bouncer and Gerry bonded well together and the three of them enjoyed each other's company. Finally, emerging from a small copse, they came to a clearing and before them, set up on an embankment and overlooking the estate, stood a small timber-framed orangery. Eloise loved the place and she recalled all the happy times she had spent there as child, with her late mother.

"This was Mummy's favourite place," she said, toying with a silver locket that hung from her neck, "I come here to be close to her."

Gerry could see why; the view over the estate was astounding, especially now, with the back-drop of the setting sun.

"What was her name?" he asked, hoping it wouldn't upset her.

"Sylvia. She was lovely, Gerry. I do miss her so."

"I'm sure she misses you just as much," he replied, taking her hand in his.

They sat in silence for a moment, enjoying the view. Yawning, Bouncer settled at their feet and, together, they watched as the sun set lower on the horizon.

"Beautiful," he said.

"Yes, it is," she agreed, smiling. She turned to face him but the smile didn't hide the sadness in her eyes, as they reflected the early evening sky, now ablaze and adorning itself with hues of oranges and reds. As he looked into her eyes, a tightness started to grow in the depths of his stomach and he knew that feeling well but hadn't felt it for a very long time. He was falling for her. He wanted to pull her into his arms, to share in her sadness. To kiss her. To love her. But now wasn't the time and maybe Eloise knew that too.

"We had best be getting back," she said. "Doris will be awfully upset if we are late for dinner."

"Of course," he replied. "I'll race you."

Bounding from the orangery, Gerry took the lead, with Bouncer hot on his heels and yelping excitedly.

"Bumble, you cheat," she shouted after him. "That's very unsporting of you. And as for you, Bouncer, you're such a traitor."

* * *

As Gerry reached the top of the steps by the fountain, he saw a van, with the words 'Ponsonby - Import and Export' stencilled on the side, parked outside the entrance to the house. Dressed in a fine suit, a burly, bald-headed, bulk of a man was loading boxes into the back. Gerry, not being one to let a lady lose, and also intrigued with the van, feigned an injury, allowing Eloise to race past in laughter.

"Come on, slow coach!" she shouted back at him.

"Right behind you," he said. "You carry on." With Bouncer still at his side, Gerry rubbed his pretend injury and watched as the man attempted to pick up a large crate.

* * *

"Need a hand?" Gerry called. "That looks heavy."

The man looked surprised and nervous with the offer of help, shook his head and turned to talk to someone out of Gerry's view.

"Are you sure?" Gerry asked, as he drew nearer.

"MacNeil, isn't it?" a voice asked.

Bouncer snarled and let out a low growl as David, who was hidden from view, slipped out from behind the van.

"Yes, that's right," Gerry replied.

"Well, we're fine," he said. "You run along. Or slide, as I know you're good at that."

"Just trying to help," Gerry said.

"And like I said, we're fine."

Ignoring him, Gerry bent down to examine the box.

"Sure looks heavy," he said.

The bald man slipped his hand inside his jacket and gripped a Colt M/1914. David touched his arm and mouthed "Nien, nicht jetzt."

"Well, I'll leave you to it, then," Gerry said. "Will you be at dinner?"

"I wouldn't miss it for the world, dear fellow," David replied. "I just hope your dress sense has improved by then."

A TIME FOR ADVENTURE

Of course Gerry knew David was right. He couldn't exactly turn up to dinner dressed as he was.

"Well, I'm sure I'll find......" he started to say.

Archie timed his appearance perfectly.

"Sorry to interrupt, sir," he said, "but I took the liberty of retrieving your belongings from your automobile."

"My automobile?" Gerry asked.

"Yes, sir," he said. "That is yours? The red one, if I'm not mistaken."

Gerry looked in awe at the car, a Kissel White Eagle. The speedster body gleamed, the red paintwork and silver trim were immaculate and its torpedo-shaped body and semi-boat-tail were perfectly streamlined. The only thing missing was a set of golf clubs that would normally sit on the footplate.

"That's the beauty," Gerry said. "Thank-you, Archie and it seems I will be dressed accordingly, gentlemen," he said. "I too will be looking forward to dinner, David, so I'll see you there."

* * *

Eloise was sitting at the foot of the stairs when Gerry finally caught up with her and Bouncer rushed forward, slobbering all over her, maybe by way of an apology for switching sides.

"What kept you?" she asked.

"I stopped to give David a hand."

"How awfully sweet of you," she said. "Especially with your latest injury but you do realise I would have won."

"Is that so?" he said. "Then let's see who gets ready for dinner first."

Eloise couldn't help but laugh, as Gerry took the stairs two at a time, leaving mistress and her faithful companion behind.

"See you at 8 o'clock sharp," she called after him.

CHAPTER THREE

Sunday 23rd September, 6.00 pm

Gerry lay on the bed, closed his eyes and listened as the clock on the mantle chimed, each ring sending him further into an R.E.M. state and dreams of another time.

One......

"Good morning, Doris," he said, as his elderly neighbour collected her milk from the doorstep. "Chilly one today, so make sure you wrap up warm."

"Aye, lad, I'm used to this weather where I come from but I'm noticing it more as I get older, mind," she said, in her deep northern accent.

"Why aye, man, so I see," Gerry mocked.

"You're a cheeky fella, Gerry MacNeil," Doris said, still laughing as she pushed her door to, shutting out the frosty morning.

Two......

"Morning, Arch. Still awake, then?" Gerry said teasingly to the night porter.

Archie was about five feet eight inches tall, with receding hair, due to the fact he always arrived to work wearing the same bedraggled baseball cap and also with a fluorescent coat to match.

"Only just, mate. Been a long night," he yawned, putting down his book and giving a long stretch, as he leaned back in the office swivel chair.

"Yes, so I can see, with the sweat you've built up there," Gerry replied, referring to Archie's underarms.

"Bollocks," Archie replied.

"Yes, no doubt they are too," Gerry said.

Archie laughed, giving Gerry a cheeky wink.

Three......

"Sorry I'm late. I overslept," Ella, the slim, brunette, receptionist said, slipping off her coat. Gerry couldn't help but notice the silver locket that hung around her neck and, as she settled into the chair, the scent from her perfume filled the air, completely vanquishing the unpleasantness of poor Archie's odour. Gerry liked Ella and some would say he acted like a father figure towards her.

"That's pretty," he said, indicating the locket.

"It was my grandmother's," Ella replied, fingering the chain. "She left it to me when she died."

Gerry could see the sadness in her eyes, so turned his attention to his newly-purchased, indigo blue, fossil watch, to check the time.

Three Ten? That can't be right, he thought, tapping its face, wondering why it had stopped.

Four......

"Gerry, you want a drink?" George asked.

"Thanks, George. And make it a double."

Gerry pulled over a high stool and sat at the bar, watching as 'Gorgeous' expertly made his espresso, not spilling a bit as he gave himself the occasional glance in the mirror behind the optics. George was a good-looking lad, aged about twenty and loved by the ladies. He was quite the charmer and would do anything for anybody.

"I see enormous Ella was late again," George said, as he handed Gerry the coffee.

"Just a few minutes, so no great shakes."

"Oh, she's got great milkshakes, that one," Pete said, in his Yorkshire accent, resting his hand on Gerry's shoulder. "And make mine a double too, Georgie boy."

"Mr. MacNeil, how the devil are you, this morning?"

Pete also pulled up a stool and sat next to Gerry. With his robust frame, ruddy complexion and exuberant mannerisms, he was often likened to Santa Claus.

"Morning, boss, you're up early today?" Gerry said, handing Pete his own coffee.

"Oh, yes, got one of those God awful directors' meetings at three ten today and a shit load of paperwork to do," Pete replied.

Three ten? That's weird, Gerry thought, remembering his watch face.

"That's a strange time," he said.

"Yes, I know. Just about when I would enjoy my afternoon tea," Pete replied.

"Tough at the top," George interrupted.

Gerry and Pete stared at him, not saying anything and George turned back to admire his own reflection once again.

Five......

"Hi, Davey," Gerry said, as he entered the Araldite-infused pro shop.

Davey, the club professional, looked up. Removing his peaked cap, he revealed his tight curls of blonde hair and smiled a wide smile.

"Hey, Gerry. How are you today?" he replied. "Won't keep you a mo."

Gerry waited, watching Davey slide a new grip firmly over another golfer's shaft, fitting it snuggly in place.

"You do know it's ladies' day, don't you?" Davey said, wiping the excess glue from his hands.

"Yes, that's cool. I'll follow on behind and see if I can get a hole in one," Gerry replied.

"You might need these, then," Davey suggested, tossing a small package in the air. "Three for a tenner," he added.

Gerry nearly dropped the pack, because there it was again. Three and ten.

"What? What do you mean?" he asked.

"Three balls for ten pounds," Davey replied. "Enjoy your game."

Six......

He swung the club in a wide arc and it felt good. The swing followed through, smashing into the ball. He knew what it would sound like if it hit the sweet spot and this was music to his ears. His eyes followed the ball as it flew into the air, hurtling down the fairway, before touching down and rolling forward along the grass.

"Perfect, bloody perfect," he said, smiling inwardly.

That's how the rest of the game went and Gerry was buzzing; he was on a high and the numbers were put deep into the back of his mind. Well, they were, until he approached the next hole.

Gerry pulled a scorecard and pencil from his back pocket and his hand hovered over it but he couldn't write, as what he saw made him stop in his tracks. The numbers seemed to fly from the card, like they were taunting him. He couldn't take his eyes away; he just focussed on them, mesmerised and oblivious to what was going on around him.

"Ten, three, ten, three...... The tenth hole, par three."

He wondered why this felt so familiar, like he had done it all before and that the numbers meant something, something important. It was then that another number entered his thoughts, as if from far away, with a feminine ring to it.

"Fore!"

Then it hit him.

Gerry awoke with a start. He sat bolt upright on the bed and looked around the room, adjusting to his surroundings. The clock on the mantelpiece was still chiming, the hands telling him it was now 7 o'clock. Only an hour had passed, yet it seemed like a decade. It was the deepest of sleeps and he felt invigorated.

They say dreams that you remember never come true, he thought. Not for Gerry though, as it seemed *his* dreams already had.

* * *

"Not bad, MacNeil. Very dapper," Gerry said, admiring himself in the mirror thirty minutes later. The slim-fitting, pin-strip, Ritz suit, fitted him perfectly, the grey bringing out the colour of his eyes. It was tailored and made to measure, unlike his work uniform, which was at least one size too big. Cautious of the bump that had now started to bruise, Gerry ran his fingers through his strawberry blonde hair, longing for some gel to keep it in place. Making do with water, he brushed it to one side, hoping the greying edges would give him a distinguished appearance.

First the car, now the clothes. He wondered if he had been here before after all, or was he at least expected? One person may know the answer.

CHAPTER FOUR

Sunday 23rd September, 7:30 pm

"You be lost, sir?" The ageing cook asked, as Gerry entered the kitchen.

"I think I am, yes," he lied. "I must have taken a wrong turn somewhere."

"Aye," she said, "it a big 'un, this ol' place, full of them there crooks n' crannies. And that's just er and er boyfriend, mind."

"I'm sorry?" Gerry asked.

"Doris!" Archie said, stepping from the shadows. "The gentleman doesn't want to hear your tittle tattles." Turning to Gerry, he said, "Pay no heed to her, sir. You know what these northern folk are like; always got a tale to tell. Now, sir, let me point you in the right direction."

"You see, my lovelies," Doris said, "it were meant to be."

"Of course. you know I wasn't really lost, don't you?" Gerry asked, as he followed Archie up the spiral stairwell, the same stairwell he was being dragged up only a few hours before.

"I beg your pardon, sir?" Archie replied.

"The car, the clothes?" he questioned.

"Yes, sir. I believe they belong to you."

"And how I got here?" Gerry asked next.

"In your car, sir," Archie said. "I saw you arrive in it earlier today, before you played golf."

"Okay, then how do you explain......"

"Here we are, sir. The dining room's just off to your left," Archie said, interrupting Gerry mid-flow. He wished Gerry a pleasant evening and disappeared rapidly back down the stairs, leaving him none the wiser.

* * *

As Gerry crossed the hallway, Eloise was just coming down the stairs. She hadn't yet noticed him, so he slowed his pace, giving her the advantage of winning. But, in reality, the advantage was all his, as he could admire her from afar.

The bias-cut dress seemed to flow as she descended the stairs, and it draped perfectly over her frame, accentuating her slender figure. The gold of the silk fell gracefully in fluted folds, which sat just below her knees, allowing Gerry a glimpse of her long, smooth legs with every step she took.

"And I thought the sunset was beautiful," he said.

"Gerry, I didn't see you," she replied, with a startled tone. "Were you spying on me?"

"I would say admiring would be more of an accurate description, because you look radiant."

Eloise blushed, as she linked her arm in his and rested her head on his shoulder.

"We had better join the others," she whispered.

*　*　*

"Gerry, or should I say Bumble? Welcome," Georgie said. "Eloise, why don't you get your young man a drink, before dinner is served?"

'Her young man.' Gerry liked that.

"Thank-you, sir. That would be lovely. Could I have a G&T?"

"Of course but, as I said before, it's Georgie. We're all friends here."

Looking around, Gerry didn't feel everyone in the room would agree with that statement.

David stood casually with his elbow resting on the mantle of the unlit fire and the lady by his side, not much older than Eloise, was made to look taller than she was by her high-heeled stilettos. With a drink in one hand, and a cigarette in the other, David nodded over at Gerry, not by way of a greeting but more of a 'that's the unwanted newcomer I was telling you about'.

"Have you met David?" Georgie asked, noticing the contact between them.

"We bumped into each other, yes."

"Gerry helped with your delivery, Daddy," Eloise said, returning with the drinks.

"Well, I offered," Gerry said. "How is the export trade these days, Georgie?"

"To be honest, it's not looking good," he said. "There's a change coming and something's......"

"Business is for the boardroom, not the dining room, darling. And who do we have here?"

"Ah, Freda, there you are and looking as lovely as ever, I see," Georgie said. "Gerry, let me introduce my wife, Freda."

Freda was an attractive lady for her age, which Gerry put around fifty. She looked elegant in her turquoise gown and she stood with a carefree confidence. Her jet black hair was cut and groomed into a bobbed style and held in place by a bejewelled headpiece that complemented her serene, nut brown eyes. Gerry took her hand and gently kissed the top.

"Mrs. Ponsonby," he said.

Freda smiled at Gerry's manners and then addressed Eloise.

"Well, it seems we have two dashing gentlemen with us this evening, Els."

Eloise had the biggest grin. She took Gerry's hand and squeezed it tight, not wanting to let go.

"We are so lucky, Freddie," Eloise said, knowing that Gerry had been accepted.

Eloise and Freda were very close and had a lot of time for each other. Of course, Freddie would never replace Eloise's mother but her father was happy. For the first time since Sylvia was taken so suddenly in a tragic caving accident, he was happy.

"Freddie, I feel awful that I was unable to make introductions earlier but I couldn't find you. Did you go out?" Eloise asked.

"Yes, dear. There was something that needed my attention," Freda replied.

Being one to appear from nowhere, Archie rang a bell, indicating dinner was about to be served and Georgie headed to the table, with Eloise and Freda flanking him. Gerry sat happily next to Eloise and opposite David, whose lady friend had long since departed.

After the meal, which was, as Gerry had imagined, a lavish spread, the gentlemen retired to the library for cognac. Deciding on a spot of fresh air, Eloise and Freda wrapped themselves in shawls to keep out the cold of the night and then took to the patio.

* * *

Eloise sighed as she stared up at the night sky, the crispness in the air adding clarity to the stars as they shone down.

"I'm so glad you like Gerry," she said. "I did from the moment I almost killed him."

"Then why the big sigh?"

"Because I'm happy and one might even say I feel content," she said. "It's strange but I feel such a deep connection with him, Freddie. Is that wrong, after such a short space of time?"

Freda thought about the first time she met Georgie and it wasn't a dissimilar night to this one, only warmer and in Paris. It was August 3rd, 1914. She was alone and sitting on the steps of Sacré-Coeur, looking out over the city, a city she loved more than any other.

"Nous sommes en guerre, Nous sommes en guerre!" an excited young Parisian was shouting, as he ran down the steps. "L'Allemagne a déclaré la guerre"

A solitary tear ran from Freda's eye.

"It's hard to believe, isn't it?" an Englishman's voice said, as he sat next to her.

Freda turned to him

"Hold me," she cried. "Please, just hold me."

Georgie took her in his arms. She buried herself into him and sobbed.

"Why? Why has Germany declared war on France?"

Bouncer brushed against Freda's leg, bringing her back from her memories. She knelt down, pulled him to her and looked up at Eloise.

"No, it's not wrong, Els," she replied. "It was meant to be."

* * *

As he savoured its flavours, the smooth, golden cognac warmed Gerry's throat. He had declined the offer of a cigar and sat watching the flames from the fire, as they licked high into the chimney flue.

"Do you hunt, MacNeil?" David asked. He was sat on the opposite side of the mantel to Gerry in an identical red, high-back chair, made from the finest soft leather. As he blew the smoke from the cigar into the air, it danced in circles above him.

"No, David, it's not something I have tried," Gerry replied.

"You should, Gerry. You would enjoy it immensely," Georgie said, joining in on their conversation. "There's nothing like the thrill of the chase to blow the cobwebs away."

"I agree, MacNeil," David said. "Don't we have one planned soon, Georgie?"

"Now, come on, David. First names," Georgie warned. "I'm not entirely sure, but I think there may be one after my trip to Scotland," he added.

David huffed, pulled hard on his cigar and stubbed it forcefully in the crystal ashtray. He blew the remaining smoke in Gerry's direction, before devouring his cognac in one gulp.

"Another, Mac......Gerry?" He faltered, showing his empty glass.

Gerry could see the anger in David's eyes, even through the smoke. Wafting it away, Gerry replied with a simple "No thanks, I'm fine."

"Is Scotland for business or for pleasure, Georgie?" Gerry asked.

As David poured his cognac, he listened with interest. He had arranged this meeting and didn't want some good-for-nothing, son of a bitch, ruining his plans. He had a lot riding on it and stood to lose thousands of pounds, if not his life. He needed this deal.

"A bit of both," Georgie replied. "It would be a shame not to get a round in while I'm there."

Georgie joined his business partner at the globe-cum-bar and offered his glass.

"Won't you be in Austria, David?" he asked.

David knew exactly what was about to happen and couldn't do anything about it. Inwardly, he was seething but, as he poured the second cognac, he tried not to show it.

"Yes, I will be," David replied, "but I can cancel."

"No, there's no need for that. Business is business, after all. Gerry, you're a golfer. Why don't you join me?"

Gerry was excited at the prospect of playing in Scotland, the true home of golf.

"It would be an honour, Georgie," he said.

David pushed the stopper back into the neck of the decanter with such force that the bar rattled. He turned and faced Gerry, looking at him with such rage.

Georgie raised his glass to Gerry's with a chink.

"Quam natum esse," he said. "It was meant to be."

Freda, having left Eloise, popped her head around the door. "Georgie, I'm going to retire for the evening. Don't be up all night, now," she said. "Gerry, I have left Eloise on the patio. Goodnight, gentlemen."

"Well, that's me told," and, with that, Georgie started to follow Freda upstairs.

"Georgie, I need to make an important call," David said after him. "There's something I need to arrange. Do you mind?"

"Be my guest, David and goodnight to you both."

Not wanting to stay with David any longer than he had to, Gerry made his excuses and left, leaving David alone to make his call.

* * *

David sat at the desk and looked at the telephone, wondering how this could all work in his favour.

"It's Steinberg. We have a problem," David said, once he was connected

"I don't have problems. I deal with them before they become a problem", the man who answered said in a calm and collective tone. "Tell me."

"Ponsonby's bringing someone else in, a Gerry MacNeil, and they're both going to Scotland. MacNeil's too nosey for my liking. He could sour the deal," David said. "Shall I take care of him?"

"Do nothing, not until the deal is done," the man replied. "I'll send Spats down to watch over things. Oh, and Steinberg?"

"Yes?"

"Keep Ponsonby's daughter close. Don't lose my collateral. I want what's coming to me," the man warned, before hanging up.

"Oh, don't worry," David said, also hanging up. "You'll get what's coming to you."

* * *

What a strange day, Gerry thought, as he wandered through the house, listening to the creaks and moans as it settled around him. So many things had happened.

Gerry's other life was nothing compared to this one. That life was run-of-the-mill, working twelve hour shifts at Rose Cottage, doing the same thing day in and day out. He had always dreamt of adventure, of travel and of falling in love but never imagined finding it in 1928, as well as all in one day.

Eloise was still on the patio when he found her, alone and bathed in moonlight. Her dress seemed to shimmer under her shawl, as she stood shivering before him. He noticed the vapours of hot breath escape her mouth and combine with the chilly night's air and knew that, now, the time was right.

"You're cold," he said, moving behind her. "Can I warm you?"

"Yes, please. I would like it if you did," she replied.

Gerry lifted the shawl and wrapped it around her shoulders. His fingers traced the contours of her neck, making her shiver again but, this time, it wasn't the cold but his touch. He ran his hands over her shoulders and down her arms, pausing for the briefest of moments to enjoy the scent of her cologne, allowing it to fill his senses. He cradled his arms around her, pulling her gently into him.

"Eloise," he wanted to say, "I'm falling in love with you."

Eloise leant back into his chest and rested her head into the crook of his shoulder. Keeping her head in place, she raised her eyes to meet his and smiled, as though she knew what he was thinking.

CHAPTER FIVE

Monday 24th September, 8.00 am

The following morning, Gerry lay in bed, listening to the water running into the bath. His clothes were strewn around the room and the bed covers were only half covering his naked torso, the rest dragging on the floor. Interlocking his fingers behind his head, Gerry stared at the bathroom door; it was slightly ajar, just enough for the steam to escape.

To name but a few, he thought about his conversations with Eloise; her father's trade, David's mysterious lady friend and, of course, his trip away.

Eloise told him that Georgie was currently exporting car parts between Germany and the United States, with the help of David, who had various contacts in the industry, and that the lady was David's secretary, apparently there with important documents which needed his signature. Eloise also told Gerry that she was happy for him to be going away. She would miss him but "it will be nice for Daddy to have some company," she had said.

* * *

A TIME FOR ADVENTURE

Eloise wiped her hand across the bathroom mirror to clear some of the steam away and, with the thoughts of what happened the previous night running through her mind, she smiled back at her reflection. She had had boyfriends before but she had never felt the way she was feeling about Gerry, especially in such a short time. It wasn't just the way he held her, or the way he cared. He made her feel alive and she was going to miss him so much when he went away. She dipped her toes into the water, making sure it wasn't too hot, before submerging herself beneath the bubbles.

* * *

Gerry got up off the bed and went to the bathroom. Leaving the door ajar hadn't really helped, as it was like a sauna in there. He felt his way to the taps, stopped the running water and stepped into the bath.

Last night, having escorted Eloise to her own bedroom, they had made plans to meet for breakfast and then go for a drive. He had a quick soak and then he made the bed, which he guessed was something he probably didn't need to do but, in his 'other' time, it's what he was used to doing. Closing the bedroom door behind him, Gerry went to meet Eloise.

CHAPTER SIX

Wednesday 3rd October, 9:30 am

At 9:30 am, just over a week later, the Rolls-Royces pulled up outside King's Cross railway station. Archie got out and opened the door, so his passengers could embark. First out was Eloise, stepping out in a lady-like manner but with sorrow in her heart, then Georgie, finely-dressed and ready to do business and, lastly, Gerry, like an excited kid going on a school trip. He wasn't excited at the prospect of leaving Eloise behind and he had begged that she come along but she had insisted he go with Georgie. Archie unloaded the cases, gave a railway porter instructions and a tip, then went off to buy the tickets.

At 9:55 am, as steam hissed from the Flying Scotsman's engine, Georgie entered the first class carriage.

"Gerry, it leaves at ten on the dot," Georgie reminded him, before smiling to himself. He hadn't seen his daughter this happy for a long time.

Gerry and Eloise held each other, wanting to leave it until the very last minute before saying goodbye.

"I love you, Gerry MacNeil," Eloise said. "Come back safe to me."

A TIME FOR ADVENTURE

"You won't be anywhere near the course, so I'm bound to be safe," he replied, "I love you, Miss Ponsonby and nothing's gonna happen to me," he added.

The slim American looked up at the station clock. At 9:58 am, and carrying a small, black, violin case, he stepped out from behind the newspaper stand. From his Fedora hat down to his black and white wingtip shoes, his clothes were of an expensive Italian design. He flicked his cigarette to one side, walked across the platform and boarded the Scotsman, before the mark had a chance to spot him.

The guard checked his twenty five years of service pocket watch, as the second hand swept behind the hour hand and, as he blew his whistle at 10:00 am on the dot, the non-stop London to Edinburgh train jolted forward. Georgie fell into his seat, Eloise shed a tear and Gerry thought he recognised a slim man carrying a violin case, walking across the platform.

* * *

Gerry joined his travelling companion in the restaurant carriage and was greeted with a steaming coffee.

"I took the liberty of ordering for you, old man," Georgie said.

Gerry thanked him and poured the contents of the china cafetière into the cups, all coloured in apple green, to match the colour of the LNER locomotive.

"Unless you wanted something a little stronger?" Georgie asked, noticing Gerry had a pre-occupied look about him.

"No....no," he replied, "this is fine."

Georgie put Gerry's look down to leaving Eloise behind, then turned to shuffle through the paperwork he had set out before him. He left Gerry to his thoughts and to gaze out at the passing scenery.

In truth, Gerry was missing Eloise; they had spent every day together since his arrival and it was hard saying goodbye. But he was thinking about the slim man. Gerry had only met a handful of people in the last week and he wasn't one of them, yet he knew him. Of that he was sure.

* * *

It was 6:15 pm when the train pulled into Edinburgh Waverley station and, during the journey, Gerry and Georgie had talked, dined, slept and explored. The conversations didn't delve too deeply into business matters; it was mostly finding out about one another. Gerry embellished the truth about his background, as he didn't feel anyone needed to know about his other life but he hated having to lie, especially to these people he had grown to love, the people that had put their trust in him.

As it hurtled northbound, Gerry had looked for the slim man along the length of the train but everything seemed as it should be; gentlemen reading the daily newspaper, mothers consoling bored children, the guard in his cabin checking the train was on time, waiters serving tea and ladies-in-waiting looking after their employer's needs. The man wasn't anywhere to be seen, so Gerry had to assume he hadn't boarded the train after all.

The slim LNER guard read the inscription on the back of his newly-acquired pocket watch, as Gerry and Georgie climbed into the back of a chauffeur-driven car that would take them to their final destination. The Hamilton Grand, Saint Andrews.

'For twenty five years of dedicated service', it read.

"Sorry, old timer but you had your time and my need was greater than yours," he said.

He lit a cigarette, picked up his violin case and casually walked over to a waiting car.

CHAPTER SEVEN

Thursday 4th October, 10.00 am

The following morning, Gerry picked up the heavy black receiver, put it to his ear and dialled the number that would connect him to Eloise, back in Surrey.

"Effingham 8674, the Ponsonby residence," Archie said.

"Archie, it's Gerry. Can I speak to Eloise, please?" Gerry said.

"Ah, Mr. MacNeil. Miss Eloise has been expecting your call. I won't keep you a moment."

Gerry could hear the excitement in the background.

"Freddie, Freddie! Gerry's on the telephone," he heard Eloise say.

"Gerry, my love, how are you? I miss you awfully. How's Daddy? How's Scotland? Was your journey okay? Oh, Gerry, I can't wait for you to come home," she said.

Gerry laughed at her excitement and told her everything she wanted to know. He informed her that they would both be back some time the next day and then, upon hanging up, he went to join Georgie in the lobby.

As Gerry approached the reception desk, the hotel clerk was leafing through a large leather-bound diary and Georgie was waving in Gerry's direction, to beckon him over.

"Here we are, sir," the clerk said. "Mr. Brown is expecting you in room three ten."

Like the mouse, before it had scurried behind the cabinet, Gerry stopped in his tracks. There they were again. Those numbers. This is too much of a coincidence, this has to be why I'm here. It must be something to do with Georgie's meeting, he thought.

"Did you manage to get through to Eloise?" Georgie asked, putting his arms around Gerry's shoulders. "Let's go for a coffee and you can tell all."

Tell you all? I have so much to tell you, Georgie, I just wish I could, he thought.

* * *

Gerry wished him well with the meeting and waited as the bell boy slid the lift doors closed, sending Georgie to the third floor. What to do now, he thought. Play golf, as that's what Georgie believed, or somehow find out what was really going on? It didn't take long to make his mind up. After all, wasn't this what he was here for?

* * *

As Gerry was putting his plan into action, Georgie stood outside room 310 and composed himself. This was a big contract that David had arranged with the Americans and Georgie couldn't afford for it to go wrong.

He knocked twice. To his surprise, the door opened immediately; it was as if the tall, slim man, who was dressed in expensive Italian clothes, had been standing waiting for the knock.

"Ponsonby. Georgie Ponsonby," Georgie said. "I'm here to see Mr. Brown."

"Come in, why don'ts ya," the man replied. "Al's been waiting for ya."

Georgie stepped past the American and into the elaborately-decorated room. Noticing another man sitting behind a large writing desk, he proceeded to greet him.

"Mr. Brown?" he asked.

"Hold it there, fella. Needs to pat ya down, first," the slim man said.

"Spats, that's no way to treat our colonial cousin," the man behind the desk interrupted. "Take a seat......Georgie. Georgie, right?"

"Yes, that's correct."

"Of course it's correct. I'm always correct, see," Brown said. "Now let's get down to business."

Georgie, normally a positive man, had attended many business meetings, and some were with very influential people, but the stout man before him, dressed in the finest clothes money could buy, was different. He didn't know if it was the scars that ran down his left cheek or the 'devil may care' look in his eyes but this man scared Georgie and he wanted this meeting to be over as quickly as possible.

* * *

A small spectacled man, with a grey beard, and a uniform that was two sizes too big, stood outside the storage room, scraping mud from a pair of golf shoes with a sharp tool. He stopped what he was doing and looked over his spectacles, as Gerry approached.

"Guid morn tae ye, sairrr," he said, in a soft Scottish accent. "Hoo can ah help ye, the day?"

"Would you mind retrieving my clubs please, Murray?" Gerry asked, noticing the man's name badge.

"Aye, sir. It'll be a wee bit quiet owt thaur for ye, the day," Murray replied. "Fog jist come doon, sairrr, thicker than mah missis' broth, it be," he added.

While Murray disappeared into the store room, Gerry looked out of the window. Ideal, he thought. This was how he had hoped it would be, as he didn't really want to be seen.

"Murray, I feel such a fool, as I've mistakenly left my key in the room," Gerry said. "Is there a quicker way to get to three ten?"

"Och aye, sairrr, that's an easy one," Murray replied, as he returned and handed Gerry his bag. "Jist follaw th' corridur doon tae th' end."

"Thanks, Murray and have this for your trouble," Gerry said, giving him a tanner. Gerry slung the bag over his shoulder, carefully slipped the sharp cleaning tool into his pocket and followed the corridor.

* * *

He emerged from the hotel's side entrance and stared up at the third floor. The fog was so dense, that Gerry was barely able see to the top of the roof. Pulling his collar up and tweed flat cap over his ears, he grabbed a club from the bag and made his assent up the iron staircase.

As he stood on the balcony overlooking the first tee, Gerry took a moment to ponder. I wonder what the view would be like on a clear summer's day, he thought. If I survive this, I'll have to come back and find out.

Gerry heard voices from inside the room but he wasn't able to see much through the thickly-netted window. Pressing himself against the damp brickwork, he made his way to the adjacent room and pushed down on the door handle, praying it wouldn't be locked. The door opened with a click and Gerry slid silently inside.

With his back now to the window, he looked through the crack in the bedroom door and could see three men; Georgie studying some paperwork, a man whose back was to Gerry and a slim man who seemed to be keeping watch, while smoking a cigarette. It was the same slim man that he had seen at the station but now Gerry had a clearer view.

Spats Spatelli, I knew it, Gerry thought to himself. Hired killer, gun for hire. Gerry remembered reading about Spatelli in one of his many books and he was so focussed on the man, that he didn't hear the rotund figure move silently behind him.

"Don't move, don't make a sound and we can all get out of here alive," he whispered, covering Gerry's mouth with his hand. Gerry did as he was told and he didn't even blink, as a hand slipped into his pocket and pulled out the sharp tool.

"What were you going to do with this, my old friend? Clean his shoes, or put scars on his other cheek?" his captor said.

Gerry knew that voice, spoken with a Yorkshire twang.

"Pete?" he mumbled.

"Ssshh, bonnie lad. Now get out of here. Meet me in the Just Inn Time mid-day, two days from now and I'll explain everything," Pete said. "Now go."

The slim American looked over at the door that adjoined the rooms, as though something had caught his attention. Putting his cigarette in the ashtray, he got up from his chair, nodding at Brown to the direction of the door. Brown waved his hand, dismissing the action, as he needed the papers signing and knew whatever Slim had heard could wait.

"Spats, why don't you get Geor......Mr. Ponsonby something to drink," Brown said.

He was a professional in his field and he knew better than to address his guests by their first name for the sake of the hired help's benefit, even if they were a first-class assassin.

"Now, Georgie, so we agree? That's fifty crates of parts and I need them in Chicago in two weeks, see," he continued.

Georgie read through the contract and Slim placed two crystal tumblers on the desk. Georgie picked up his glass and sipped the warming Scotch whisky.

"Everything looks in order, so yes, fifty," he said. "I'll just sign these and be on my way."

"And I thought you Brits did everything at a leisurely pace," Brown said.

"Places to go, people to see and all that, old bean."

Brown laughed at the British etiquette and handed Georgie a pen.

"Okay, okay, I get ya," he said. "Now sign ya life away."

With the contract signed, Georgie downed the rest of the whisky and the two men shook hands to complete the deal.

"Let me see you out," Brown said. "Slim, why don't you see to the other business?"

* * *

Pete stood behind the door, waiting. He picked up the club that Gerry had left behind and was ready to swing. The door opened slowly, as Spats came through holding his 9 mm Browning hand gun before him. The club head swung through the air, landing full force on Spats' outstretched arm, sending the gun flying under the bed. Spats was quick but not quick enough. For a man of his build, Pete moved deftly and side-stepped Slim's charge, swinging the club in a way any golfer would be proud of. Bringing it up with the perfect follow-through, the club head struck home, connecting solidly under his chin. As blood sprayed from his mouth, Spats was lifted off the ground and he flew backwards, crashing into the door and collapsing against it in a heap. With the door blocked, Pete had time to retrieve the gun and escape the way he had come in but not before leaving a calling card.

The door was being pushed open from the other side, as Spats started to come round. With his head spinning, and the taste of blood fresh in his mouth, he pulled himself up.

"Spatelli, you dumb guinea schmuck," Brown said. "Who was it? Who did this?"

Spats grabbed hold of the now open door and tried to stay upright.

"I don't know. He was too quick," he replied. "You wants me to go after him?"

Brown didn't reply. He walked over to the bed, picked something up and returned to his desk, ignoring Spats completely.

* * *

Picking up the ivory-encrusted receiver, he held it to his ear and dialled. At the other end of the line, the ring of the telephone reverberated around an old converted barn, situated somewhere on the Kelsey Hall estate. David grabbed the dusty receiver on the third ring.

"Steinberg, it's Capone. Al Capone."

"Mr. Capone!" David said.

"Get the girl," Capone instructed.

"The girl? Of course. Did the deal go down?"

"Yes…yes, the deal's done. Just get the girl, see."

"What about MacNeil?" David asked.

"His time will come," Capone said. He calmly replaced the receiver in its cradle and studied the miniature, silver-topped, walking cane he had picked up off the bed. He twisted it between finger and thumb. "Peter Dann, the Secret Intelligence Service's finest," he said to himself. "So we will get to meet again, you limey son of a bitch." He traced the tip of the cane along the length of his scars, the cold of the silver against his skin reminding him of the time they last met. Reminding him just how cold and ruthless Peter Dann could be.

David also replaced his receiver and then brushed the dust from his hands.

"Schmidt, get the truck ready," he said. "We're going to Kelsey Hall, first thing.

CHAPTER EIGHT

Friday 5th October 6:30 am

The following morning, Eloise leafed through the daily paper as she sat alone by the patio door, while enjoying her tea, toast and marmalade breakfast. It was her favourite time of the day and she would often get up early, before riding her favourite gelding across the estate. She could take in the quietness of the house whilst everyone else slept, a time to gather her thoughts and be at one with her own company, in the knowledge that she wouldn't be disturbed.

As she scanned the pages, one particular headline caught her eye.

FLYING SCOTSMAN'S RAIL GUARD FOUND GAGGED AND BOUND

Police appeal for witnesses travelling on Wednesday, 3rd October, on the London to Edinburgh train, to come forward if they saw anything suspicious during their journey.

If it wasn't for the occasional cloud cover dropping the temperature a degree or two, she would have been out on the patio enjoying the sunrise and then maybe she would have seen him coming.

A TIME FOR ADVENTURE

The large man grabbed her from behind, smoothing her mouth with a chloroform-soaked cloth. She instinctively kicked out, sending the small breakfast table toppling, as she was lifted with ease from the chair. She tried with every ounce of strength to fight back but he was too strong. Her arms were pinned and, as she was dragged away, no-one could hear her muffled screams. The last image Eloise had before the drug took hold, and darkness enveloped her, was of a photograph fluttering to the floor.

* * *

In Edinburgh, the sun had long since broken the horizon and, as the whistle blew at 10:00 am, the Flying Scotsman once more started its journey. This time, southbound and homeward, they both had their own reasons for wanting to leave Scotland so eagerly; Gerry to get back to Eloise, and Georgie, purely so he could complete his part of the deal and have nothing to do with Mr. Brown again.

Gerry had said nothing of his encounters on the third floor the previous day, or of the fact that Peter had shown up. All Georgie needed to know was that his make-believe golf card was impressive and likewise, but for the sake of pride more than anything else, Georgie didn't tell Gerry that he may have unwittingly made a deal with the devil himself.

CHAPTER NINE

Friday 5th October, 7.00 pm

"Who would do such a thing, Georgie?" Freda sobbed.

Gerry stood by the library fire, the flames doing nothing for his feeling of angst, as he watched Georgie console his stricken wife. This isn't fair on them, I have to say something, Gerry thought.

"I know what you're thinking, Gerry," Archie said "but now's not the time."

Gerry turned, surprised to see Archie by his side.

"So you do know something?" he whispered.

"Yes but, for the sake of national security, this has to remain quiet."

He was too concerned about Eloise to worry about the nation or its security.

"Where's Eloise. Is she safe?"

"That, I don't know. Follow me. I have something to show you."

A TIME FOR ADVENTURE

They walked the length of the entrance hall towards the spiral stairwell, wanting to be out of earshot of Georgie and Freda and then Archie handed Gerry a photograph of Eloise, with a hand written note on the back.

"Read this," he said. "I retrieved it before the master and lady found it, it was meant for you Gerry."

'I HAVE YOUR SWEETHEART. NO HARM WILL COME TO HER, IF YOU DO EXACTLY AS I SAY.

ON OCTOBER 11TH THE GRAF ZEPPELIN WILL FLY FROM FRIEDRICHSHAFEN. BE ON IT WITH £50,000.

DON'T ALERT THE POLICE.

A.C.'

By the time they reached the kitchen, Gerry had read the note many times over.

"I don't understand. Why me and who's AC?"

"Al Capone."

Gerry stopped reading and looked at Archie in disbelief.

"Al Capone? *The* Al Capone?"

"The very same but we both know he didn't sign it, don't we?"

Gerry looked back at the initials, and of course he knew.

"David, right?" he asked.

"Yes, one and the same. David Steinberg, gun runner extraordinaire."

Gerry thought back to the van and the boxes that were being loaded. David was using the export business to supply guns to the Mafia. Now it was starting to make sense.

"But why sign it as Capone?" he asked.

Archie stayed silent for a long time.

"To incriminate him, Gerry," he said, finally. "I can't tell you any more than that. When you meet with Peter, everything will become clear."

CHAPTER TEN

Saturday 6th October, 12 noon

The rain hadn't stopped since he left Kelsey Hall five miles back. It was the sort of rain that blew from every direction, soaking through the skin of anyone foolish enough to venture out. Gerry sat staring through the windscreen, the single wiper swishing rapidly from side to side, allowing him the occasional glimpse of the King's Head public house, the sound of the rain cascading onto the vinyl roof only delaying the inevitable. He knew he had to make a dash for it. Running head down across the car park, he was drenched by the time he reached the pub's entrance.

"Why don't you look where you're going?" the woman huffed, as Gerry bolted into the porch way, knocking her sideways.

He bent down, picking her umbrella up from the wet cobbled floor. Noticing her stilettos, he wondered why on earth anyone would wear heels in such weather.

"I'm – I'm sorry. I was trying to get in from the rain," he said.

She didn't reply. With her features disguised by a silk headscarf, she snatched the umbrella and stepped out into the downpour, briefly looking back, as Gerry entered the pub.

A TIME FOR ADVENTURE

* * *

He wasn't the only foolish one that day, as the bar was packed. The odour of damp Burberry trench coats that were hung to dry by the raging log fire, fermented yeast and stale smoke, filled the air, sending a wave of nausea over him.

"MacNeil. Gerry MacNeil."

Gerry scanned the bar, finding it difficult to see where the shouts were coming from, amidst the throngs of village locals and young farmhands who were enjoying some respite from their daily routine.

"Over here, Gerry." Wearing an olive, country check, three-piece suit, a garish tie that hung loosely below his unbuttoned collar and breeches tucked into his hunting boots, Peter stood in the open doorway, his frame almost filling the entirety of the gap.

Eventually spotting him, Gerry made his way across the bar, carefully stepping over a slumbering sheepdog, as it lay loyally at its master's muddy feet. The farmer tipped his cap as Gerry passed.

"Two of your finest, if you please, landlord," Peter said, as he closed the door behind them.

The room was small, the floorboards well-trodden and the floral wallpaper was yellow from years of smoke. The frosted glass, set above head height in the door, had the mirror image of the letters SNUG etched into it and, in a roundabout way, spelled GUNS. With the sounds of the bar now muffled, Gerry took a seat by the window which, like the door, was also frosted, giving them total privacy. Peter sat opposite, placing a silver-topped cane across the table and pushing two empty glasses to one side. He took Gerry's hand and shook it.

"I expect you have lots of questions for me, my old friend," he said.

Some, Gerry thought, as he looked back at his boss. Was he his boss, still? He still looked the same, having not changed over the years, or was it days? Maybe even hours? Gerry had no idea. This time travel stuff was all new to him.

"So Pete, I can travel in time?"

"Well, not in the ordinary sense, no," Peter replied, releasing his grip.

"Ordinary? What's ordinary about it?" Gerry asked. "Don't get me wrong, I bloody love it. It's – just – how shall I put it? I don't seem to know my arse from my elbow, right now."

"Same old Gerry," Peter said, laughing. "Always able to make light out of a bad situation."

He knew Peter was right, of course, and it *was* how he dealt with difficulties. But, up until now, none had been this difficult.

"Is it bad? I mean with Eloise. She will be okay, won't she?" he asked.

Peter saw the concern in his friend's eyes.

"I hope so, Gerry, truly I do. Are you okay?"

"I've been better but nothing a beer wouldn't put right," Gerry replied with a wink.

"Ah, yes, the beers," Peter smiled. "Let me chase them up."

Gerry twisted the stem on one of the empty glasses between his fingers, while he waited. The one with the red lipstick, still fresh on its rim. His memory flashed back to the stilettos, the same stilettos David's lady friend had worn that first night he saw her.

"I got us a whisky chaser," Peter said on his return. "Thought you might need it."

Sitting back in his chair, Gerry swallowed the whisky in one gulp, deciding to use the beer as a chaser instead. He sat and he listened.

A TIME FOR ADVENTURE

"Everyone travels in time at least once, if not more, during their life. I have many times before," Peter said. "It's the feeling of doing something, or of being somewhere, and knowing for certain you've done it or been there before."

"Déjà vu?"

"Yes, déjà vu," Peter replied. "The mind takes a snapshot as times are switched, just the briefest of memories. Imagine the mind playing a slideshow of the events that occurred on the journey and it falters for a second or two. That's déjà vu and that's the moment you traverse from one time to another."

"Okay, you have my attention," Gerry said, as he leaned closer, in the hope that doing so would make it become clearer.

"This is where it gets complicated," Peter continued, "as only a part of the traveller leaves their other self and only in that moment of déjà vu. It's like leaving a fingerprint in time."

Gerry thought for a moment.

"But I've been here for over a week," he said.

"Time is infinite, Gerry. You may be here for ten weeks, ten years even but, in 1994, you had that snapshot, you came here, left a fingerprint and now your other self is carrying on as normal."

"So can I change history?" Gerry asked. "Make the world a better place?"

"No. What has happened has happened. The past is behind us and that can't be changed."

Peter paused a moment, taking a sip of whisky. "That's better, why don't you try yours, Gerry."

"I can't, I've already drank mine......Oh, I see. It's already happened."

"Exactly. You can't change it," Peter said, smiling. "But Gerry ..."

"Yes?"

"Time twists but the outcome always remains the same."

"Twists?"

"Think of it as a scenario. Imagine you're in a boat and on a collision course with the Titanic. You hit it and the ship sinks." Peter demonstrated the actions, using two empty glasses. "You've heard the saying, what will be, will be?"

"Something to do with fate?" Gerry replied, with a puzzled look.

"Yes, it was the Titanic's fate that it sunk and the fate of all those poor souls. It was meant to be but, in history, the history you remember, it still hit an iceberg."

"Then what's the point?"

"There is no point, that's the beauty of it. Whatever you do in this time, no matter how bizarre, it can't change what has already happened. It's your free pass to adventure, Gerry.

"And if I complete what I'm here to do, what then?" Gerry asked.

"You go back. Back to your other self and all this will become that moment of déjà vu."

"And Eloise, what will become of her? Will she just be a fleeting moment in my memory?"

"I'm afraid so my friend, she's from this time and will continue her life as destiny sees fit."

Gerry stood up and paced the room, weighing everything up. He stopped suddenly and looked in Peter's direction.

"What about numbers?" he asked. "Numbers have a part in all this, don't they?"

"A big part, as we found numbers are the trigger to why travelling occurs," Peter replied.

"We?" Gerry questioned, picking up the lipstick-stained glass. "Is she part of the 'we'?"

"Miranda? Yes, she is, as is Archie."

"So do you control time?" Gerry asked.

"No, not at all," Peter replied. "I'm as uncertain of how or why as you are, my friend."

"Then who?"

Peter simply shrugged his shoulders in reply.

Gerry placed both hands flat on the table, hanging his head as another wave of nausea swept over him. He was drained, physically and mentally drained. The alcohol on an empty stomach didn't help and, as Peter continued, Gerry took his seat once more.

"Miranda Love works with me," Peter said. "She's on a covert operation with the pretence of being Steinberg's secretary. We've had our eye on him for some time now and we know he's got something planned. Something big."

"And this is the bit where you tell me it's got something to do with my numbers and that's the reason I'm here, right?" Gerry asked. "Do you know what he's planning?"

"I'm afraid we don't, Gerry. But whatever it is, you're right. You are connected."

"I'll do whatever it takes, Pete. I need to make sure Eloise is safe."

Peter slipped a hand inside his jacket, pulled out the Browning he had at the hotel and slid it across the table towards Gerry. "Then you're going to need this," he said.

Gerry stared at the gun, unsure what to say. The only time he had used a gun was at the fair and, even then, the unhappy stall holder had to duck. The most dangerous item Gerry had ever held was a nine iron.

Peter downed the rest of his whisky and got up to leave. Picking up his cane, he used it to inch the gun closer to Gerry.

"You *will* need it, "he said. "David Steinberg's a dangerous man."

Gerry turned his attention from the gun and eyed Peter, not realising until then just how powerful his friend looked as he towered over him.

"I'm sure we will speak again soon," the large man said, then left Gerry alone in the Snug, with not only a weight on his shoulders but also a gun in his hands.

CHAPTER ELEVEN

Saturday 6th October, 2.00 pm

She watched as Peter left the pub and crossed the car park, doing his best to dodge the potholes which were full with rainwater from the downpour, which had now eased to a drizzle.

"Do you think he's up to it?" she asked, as Peter climbed into the passenger seat next to her.

"I really do hope so, my dear," Peter replied. "I really do."

Miranda Love removed the headscarf and her hair fell freely over her shoulders and down her back. Pulling a red lipstick and a mirror from her handbag, she applied a fresh coat to her subtle lips, enhancing them and making them seem fuller.

"And if he isn't, what then?" she asked, still looking at her reflection, as she puckered her lips and rolled them together.

Peter took his time to answer. He watched admiringly, wondering why she needed make-up to mask her natural beauty. Only he knew it but Peter loved Miranda.

"Then God save us all," he said, finally turning away from her.

A TIME FOR ADVENTURE

Miranda started the car and let it run idle.

"Where to?" she asked.

"London, I think."

She put the car into gear, revved the engine, released the brake and then let the car roll forward. Miranda revelled in the feeling of power she had while being in control of the Mercedes Gazelle, throwing it around the country lanes, pushing it to its limits and often reaching speeds of 100 mph, with the help of the supercharger clutch. It wasn't only the power but the freedom she felt, as the wind rushed through her long blonde hair. As she sped from the car park, leaving the King's Head in their wake, Miranda caught a glimpse in the rear view mirror of someone standing in the pub's entrance, staring after them.

Gerry watched as the cream sportster left the car park and accelerated at speed towards London. The rain trickled down his face, as he thought about his own agenda and the direction he should head. To Kelsey Hall and the whereabouts of Eloise.

* * *

"It be on the change, that it be."

Startled, Gerry turned in the direction of the countrified voice. The farmer stood in the entrance of the pub, looking down the length of his clay pipe at Gerry. He shielded it from the wind, puffing hard, trying to get it to light as his dog, still obedient, sat at his feet, while staring up at its master with an 'is it time to go home yet' look on its face.

"I'm sorry?" Gerry asked

"The weather. It be on the change, ol'rite."

"Ah, yes, it seems to be clearing up," Gerry said, looking at the sky, which showed signs of blue through the breaking clouds.

"Ay, lots of clearing up coming, if truth be told," the farmer replied.

"Well, nice talking to you," Gerry said, not wanting to appear rude, "but I must be heading back."

The farmer tapped his pipe against the wall, emptying its smouldering contents onto the wet floor, before tipping his cap.

"Ay, ya back. Watch ya back, laddie," he said, turning away from Gerry. "It was meant t' be."

"What? What do you mean?" Gerry asked but the farmer walked on, seeming not to hear. "Come on, boy. Let's be getting ya back in time for tea," he said, patting his dog on the head.

Gerry wondered if he was mistaken, as he watched the pair disappear around the back of the pub. Maybe he hadn't heard right, or were the words 'it was meant to be' just another coincidence?

CHAPTER TWELVE

Saturday 6th October, 2:45 pm

"Gerry. Thank God," Georgie said. "Archie told me you went to see PD. Does he know what's happened to Eloise? Does he know where she is? Does – does he know anything, anything at all?"

Georgie had aged, Gerry thought. In that short space of time, poor Georgie seemed older. He sat in the high-back leather chair where, just over a week before, in that very room, he had been the proverbial host. Now, with his head in his hands, he looked a broken man.

"It was meant to be," Gerry said, without answering Georgie's own questions. He paused, just long enough to see what reaction it would receive.

Georgie looked up with a puzzled look, curious as to the question.

"Does that mean anything to you?" Gerry continued.

"Yes, of course. It's our family motto," he answered. "When my grandfather first saw this place, he fell in love with it and that's what he said. Quam natum esse. But what does that have to do with Eloise?"

Gerry wondered the same thing.

"I'm not sure."

Not knowing what to do for the best, but knowing he couldn't do anything alone, Gerry pulled the ransom photo from his pocket and handed it to Georgie.

"Read this," he said.

As he studied the writing, a heavy silence befell the room. Gerry waited, unsure of what response to expect.

"I'm coming with you."

"What?"

"To Friedrichshafen, I'm coming with you, Gerry. If fifty thousand pounds means getting my daughter back safely, then let the bastard have it. Eloise is worth much more than that."

The sudden change in Georgie was, in a way, frightening. As he rushed to the desk and picked up the telephone, there was anger in his eyes and a determination in his looks. "Operator, get me the Bank of England. And hurry," he said.

CHAPTER THIRTEEN

Sunday 7th October, 3:15 pm

When she first woke up, her head was pounding and she felt nauseous. Now sore from cries of help, a bad taste was in the back of her throat and her airways were full of a sweet, yet pungent, smell. But that was hours ago; at least, it felt like hours. Eloise had no sense of time in that dark room, as she pulled the course blanket over her body, covering herself completely to help keep the chill from her bones, wishing Gerry was there to protect her. The sound of rain cascading onto a roof somewhere above made her thankful that at least it was dry, wherever she was.

With her initial fears of being abducted now subsiding, Eloise knew she needed to explore; she had to learn her surroundings and use that knowledge to her advantage. Years of caving with Sylvia, her mother, had taught her to embrace the unknown.

Doing the best she could to keep the blanket in place, Eloise waved an outstretched arm tentatively into the darkness. As she ran a hand along its length, the brickwork to her right felt cold and the open space before her seemed clear. Leaving the safety of a makeshift mattress that offered little comfort, she edged forward. The floor was rough and cobbled, hurting her knees as she crawled but, thankfully, her jodhpurs and riding boots saved any grazing.

Keeping as close to the wall as she could, for fear of falling into some unknown chasm, Eloise found her path blocked by what appeared to be wooden crates. She leaned against the stack, testing their overall weight. The crates were heavy; they wouldn't topple. Using them for leverage, Eloise reached to the top, pulling herself up and onto her feet. Resting against the crates, she thought for a moment, before moving on. If the room was used for storage, there had to be a light switch. There just had to be. Like a climber on a cliff's edge, she side-stepped along the crates with her back pressed firmly against them, keeping away from the imaginary precipice and the void that might lie below.

It wasn't long before she reached the end of the row and, as she rounded the corner, a hint of light became visible, seeming to float like an illuminated L just above her line of vision. It was only a glimmer but it was still enough to give Eloise hope.

She took a step towards the light, braving the fall if it were to come. It didn't. The ground was still solid beneath her feet. Strangely, the feeling of hope gave Eloise a new warmth, allowing her to shrug the blanket to the floor and continue on. With her arms outstretched once again, as if trying to reach for the light itself, her hands touched two wooden rails, fixed solidly to the walls. Gripping the rails, Eloise began to climb a narrow staircase and, with each step she took, the light grew nearer, until eventually the source was revealed.

Eloise sat on the top step and traced her finger along the lines of light that formed the L. A warm draught filtered through the gap in the wall, bringing with it the faintest of smells, a smell that was somehow familiar but, with the after-effects of the chloroform still lingering in her nose, she couldn't quite place it.

Moving her head close to the wall, Eloise pressed her ear to the gap and listened for any sounds that might lie beyond. For a moment, there was nothing, just an eerie silence that sent shivers down her spine, with the realisation that she was totally alone. Alone that was, until a scratching sound, low down and within the wall, broke the silence. Eloise cupped her ear, as if doing so would amplify the sound.

"Hello," she whispered. "Is anyone there?"

The scratching stopped as suddenly as it had started.

"Hello," Eloise repeated.

Silence.

"Can you hear me? I'm locked in here," Eloise continued.

More silence.

She wondered if whoever was there was also a prisoner. Someone sharing her fate but in a jail which was warm and brightly lit.

"Can you help me?" she asked.

The scratching continued again, as though deliberately ignoring her plea.

Feeling defeated, Eloise moved back, sagging against the stairway wall. As she sat looking at the slither of light, hoping it would swallow her up and lead her to safety, she noticed what looked like paper wedged into the gap and, fingering it loose, it became apparent that it was in fact an envelope. As she tried in vein to read the writings scrawled on its surface, an unexpected chill swept over her. It seemed to come from the darkness below, like a draught when a door is opened. Without time to read any more than '*My darling granddaughter...*' Eloise stuffed the envelope quickly into her boot, keeping it safe and out of sight of her captor. Suddenly, a blinding light filled the room, forcing her eyes to automatically shut tight. Footsteps and the sound of voices followed, causing Eloise to sit deathly still. As did the mouse, that had stopped scratching and now, poking its head through the gap in the wall, it quickly backed away, retreating into the safety of the hole when the gruff voice echoed up the stairs.

"Get down here, now," The large man that stood at the foot of the stairs said. "Schnell." He continued, glaring up at Eloise, the gun in his hand pointing directly at her.

"You!" she said. "I know you, your David's......" Her voiced trailed off when she saw him.

"David!"

"Do as he says, Els. Quietly now and you won't get hurt."

Glad of the light, so she didn't have to feel her way, Eloise descended the stairs and stood, feeling minuscule before the gun-toting German.

"Why?" she asked, addressing David.

"Let's just say I'm shaping the world for a better future, shall we, Els?"

"A better future for who? You?" she asked. "Daddy won't give you anything." Of course, she knew that that wasn't true but it gave her a few extra seconds to look for an escape route, while David laughed at her comment.

"Els, my dear Els, indeed he will and we both know that. But Daddy is an insignificant part of my plan."

"Your plan? You mean you actually have a plan?" she said, goading him, wanting him to get rattled. She knew him well enough to know it wouldn't take much. "Or is someone else pulling your strings?" she added.

"You snooty bitch!" He grabbed Eloise by the shoulders, pulled her towards him and she could feel his hot breath, as he spoke into her ear.

"The third Reich, Els. That is the future. A superior race is in the making. Just one man stands in my way Els. Church......" His voice stopped suddenly.

Eloise had heard enough and she seized the moment.

"Don't you bloody well call me Els!" she screeched.

David was caught off-guard. She raised her knee, slamming it hard into his groin. In the split second if took for David to buckle in agony, Eloise had pulled her discarded blanket from the floor, swished it through the air and landed it squarely over the German's head, momentarily blinding him. The gun fired. Eloise ducked involuntarily but it didn't stop her plight for freedom.

"And this! This is for calling me snooty," she said. Making for the open door, her fist came into contact with David's nose, as she dashed past him. Flicking the light off, she left her captors behind, struggling in the darkness.

Another shot rang out. Eloise ran full pelt down the long, dimly-lit tunnel, as the sound of the bullet bounced off the concave walls around her.

* * *

"What was that?" Gerry said. "Was that a gunshot?"

Georgie put the receiver in its cradle and went to the window. The fresh air on his face was welcoming, as he pushed the frame open. He listened.

"It was probably old farmer Cyril, out hunting with his dog," he said.

Gerry wasn't convinced.

"But it sounded so close," he said, pulling the door to the entrance hall open. He stood by the staircase and looked in every direction. Georgie followed and they stood silently together, as if expecting a masked gunman to reveal himself at any moment.

'BANG' The sound of the second gunshot reverberated throughout the house.

"That was definitely inside. It came from the kitchen," Gerry said. He looked towards the spiral stairwell and then, as if looking at their own reflections, both men turned in unison and faced each other.

"Eloise!!" they said.

Gerry was first to enter the kitchen, with Georgie close behind. Nothing. The kitchen was empty.

"It was down here," Gerry said. "I'm sure of it."

"This house is large, Gerry. It could have come from anywhere," Georgie told him.

"No, it was here....but... ." Something caught Gerry's eye.

The mouse emerged from behind the dresser and, as if oblivious to their presence, it ran across the floor, passing them both, before disappearing into the scullery.

Gerry hurried to the dresser and studied it. Made from solid oak, it sat against the wall and reached from floor to ceiling. It looked heavy. Immovable. He waited, listening.

"Come on, let's look outside," Georgie suggested. He turned to leave.

"Wait! I hear something. It's voices," Gerry said. "Behind here."

* * *

Now free of the blanket, the German felt around in the dark, searching for David, to help him to his feet.

"Get after her!" David attempted to shout, breathlessly.

"Jawohl!" the German replied, leaving David to cradle his injured groin. He followed the lights to the tunnel and gave chase.

Eloise ran as fast as she could. The 'THUMP, THUMP' of footsteps chasing her seemed to be gaining, making her up the pace, as the end of the tunnel came into view. She leapt up a small set of concrete steps and entered a large room which was filled with an assortment of boxes and crates. Slowing to a halt, Eloise scanned the room. She knew it wouldn't be long before David and his henchman would be upon her but the only way out was blocked. With its back doors open, the Ponsonby delivery van sat in the exit, stopping her escape.

"Stop, or I'll shoot!" the German demanded.

Eloise turned to face him. Again, the gun was trained on her and she could just make out the figure of David emerging from the tunnel, hobbling and carrying a rope.

"Tie her up and put her in the van," he said, tossing the rope to the German. "And gag her too, this time," he added.

Eloise knew there was no escape and she allowed herself to be bound.

"You stupid fool. Gerry will get you for this, he'll find you and……." she said, as the gag halted her mid-flow and she was hoisted into the back of the van. David then slammed the doors shut, locking her inside.

"I'm sure he will, Els," she heard him say. "No doubt he's knocking the walls down right this minute."

* * *

Grabbing one end, Gerry pulled at the dresser to see if it would budge. It gave a little, rocking gently, causing the crockery to rattle on the shelves.

"I think it's a false wall," he said to Georgie. "There must be a release mechanism."

"There is indeed, sir," Archie said, as he mysteriously appeared in the kitchen.

"Archie!" Georgie said, surprised. "Is Freda okay?"

"She's gone to stay at her parents, sir, as you requested. I thought it best if I sent Doris home too," he replied.

"Good man! Now let's get this wall open."

A TIME FOR ADVENTURE

"There's a catch just about .... here," Archie said, as he ran his hand between the wall and the dresser.

With a click, its lock was released and the dresser sprang forward, creaking on invisible hinges. The three men stepped away as it swung open. Automatically triggering a switch, a light came on, illuminating their path. Gerry led the way and they descended the stairs, entering what was earlier Eloise's prison, now vacant of the voices Gerry had heard only moments before.

"Eloise was here," he said, spotting the blanket and mattress. It angered him, knowing someone, namely David, had imprisoned Eloise there, right under her family's nose. Gerry pulled the Browning from his pocket and pointed it into the tunnel. "This way," he said.

Surprised to see the gun, but not saying anything, Georgie followed. Less surprised, Archie joined them, producing his own firearm, a small 25 Colt automatic pistol.

"You too?" Georgie said.

Archie shrugged. "I'll explain later." He said.

* * *

They were too late. As they emerged from the tunnel, the van was pulling away and Georgie recognised it immediately as the Ponsonby delivery van. What he didn't expect to see was David sitting in the passenger seat, as it disappeared from view.

"I think someone needs to tell me what's going on here," he said. "Why has David taken my daughter?" He turned to face Gerry and Archie for an answer.

"He's not exactly who you think he is," Archie replied.

Georgie pointed to Archie's gun. "It seems as much can be said about the pair of you."

Archie holstered his Colt and went to an open crate labelled 'Car parts - destination USA.'

"Your so-called partner had a little business of his own going on, sir." He reached into the crate, dug beneath the parts and pulled out a Thompson machine gun. He handed it to Georgie, then went on to explain everything.

Gerry stood to one side, listening, thinking how strange it was that, after all that had happened, Archie still referred to Georgie as 'sir'. That's loyalty for you, he thought.

Still cradling the machine gun, Georgie looked at them both in disbelief.

"Time travel! You – you're time travellers?"

"Yes, sir, that's correct, as was your father."

"My father?"

"Yes, I was just a stable lad back then, unaware of such things. But your grandfather knew, he told me I had an important part to play in the future, that things had to be put right, so he took me under his wing and taught me all he knew. Then he had the secret wall and all this installed," Archie explained, waving his arms around the room. "I remember him saying that one day it would be needed, that it was meant to be."

"As is our family motto," Georgie said.

"Exactly, sir, and it all seems to be connected with what Steinberg has planned."

"So whatever it is, David's using Capone as a scapegoat?" Gerry asked.

"Correct," Archie replied.

"What about my daughter? We need to get her back."

"And that we will, sir. Steinberg doesn't know we're on to him yet and we know just where he's going to be."

"Friedrichshafen," Gerry said.

Georgie thought for a moment, studying the machine-gun. He placed it back in the crate. "That will never do," he said.

"But, sir....."

"I think something a little less conspicuous would be much more appropriate, don't you?"

He picked up a small hand gun, cocked it and fired at the empty space where the van had been.

"Let's go get my daughter," he said.

CHAPTER FOURTEEN

Monday 8th October, 11:20 am

Gerry found the drive to London pleasant enough; no queues on the M25 and no low emission or congestion charges. An hour's drive straight up Stane Street, or the A24 as it would be known in the future, and he was crossing the Thames over London Bridge. It had been decided the previous morning that Archie would stay at Kelsey Hall and make their travel arrangements, while Gerry and Georgie headed to the city.

"Has it changed much?" Georgie asked.

"Well, it still looks like me," Gerry replied, as he studied the photo in his new passport, which Archie had also arranged.

"No. London, I mean," Georgie replied. "One would imagine this all looks different to what it does in your time."

"Ah yes, but when exactly is my time Georgie?" he asked.

Braking sharply, Georgie steered the car toward the curb, much to the annoyance of the car behind. The driver pressed the air horn, sounding a 'HONK HONK.' "Buffoon!" he shouted, waving a fist in the air as he passed.

A few minutes later, they were leaning against the concrete railing of the bridge, looking out over the river. Full with excited passengers, the Crested Eagle paddle steamer sailed below, its telescopic funnel lowered, allowing it to pass unscathed under the bridge's arch. The smoke from the oil burner billowed into the air, smothering the two onlookers.

"This is my time, Georgie," Gerry said, romancing the idea.

"Why? What makes you so sure?"

"I don't know. Maybe everything. From the moment I arrived and met Eloise to what I'm destined to do here, whatever that is. But there's one thing I know for sure, Georgie."

"What's that?"

"Your grandfather was right; it really was meant to be." Gerry turned and looked at the car, parked haphazardly in the road. "I'm just so glad traffic wardens haven't been introduced yet, with the way I'm parked," he said. The quizzical look from Georgie made Gerry laugh. "I'll fill you in on the way to the bank, then I must pay Peter Dann a visit."

* * *

He tucked the hand-drawn map back into his pocket, grateful for Archie's directions. PO Box 500 was a grey, non-descript looking building. Walking in its shadow, the average passer-by would never know it was the headquarters of one of the most formidable intelligence agencies in the world.

Once Gerry was inside, the sharply-dressed, weasel-looking woman eyed him suspiciously, as she took his name and directed him to the tenth floor. Looking down at him over her wire-framed spectacles, she seemed quite happy to inform him that the lift was out of order. A mechanical failure, she had said. Gerry took the stairs and followed the signs to Department T, stepping to the side as throngs of workers descended upon him, escaping the confines of their offices as lunchtime approached.

The final sign, labelled 'DT' and with an arrow pointing to the left, told Gerry he was almost at his destination. He followed the empty corridor, silent now but for the tuneful whistle of 'Yankee Doodle' coming from the slim, overall-clad repairman, as he stepped into the lift. As he passed, Gerry glanced in, just as the doors were closing. Spats Spatelli stared back at him, smiling. "BOOM" he mouthed, signalling an explosion with his arms. As the doors closed completely, and the lift started its decent, Gerry was lifted from his feet.

The shockwave from the blast sent him crashing hard against the wall. Shards of glass and clumps of timber showered down, covering him as he lay dazed on the floor. As Gerry came to his senses, it took him a moment to realise what had happened. Getting to his feet, he stood surveying the carnage, as the ringing in his ears finally subsided, giving way to the crackle of fire. Luckily, the explosion itself had extinguished most of the flames, leaving small, burning embers in its wake.

He entered Department T, treading his way carefully across the debris-strewn room. Desks and chairs, tipped upside down or in pieces, lay everywhere. No longer capable of writing official memorandums, a typewriter had embedded itself in what remained of the far wall which, through the settling dust, Gerry could just make out the silhouette of Big Ben, now visible through the gaping hole.

"Is anyone here?" Gerry called, not sure who might have been in the room. A desk that was leaning against a wall suddenly fell over, sending even more dust into the air.

"Miranda. Is Miranda okay?" Peter emerged from under the desk, coughing.

"Peter!" Gerry said, rushing to his friend's aid. "Are you okay?"

"I'm fine. Shaken but stirred," he replied. "Miranda?"

Gerry looked past Peter at the pair of motionless, stiletto-clad feet, Miranda, bloodied and buried beneath the rubble. "I'm sorry," he said.

A TIME FOR ADVENTURE

Promising to avenge him for his loss, Gerry left Peter with the ambulance services and made his way from the bomb-torn building. Already, the street was crowded with gossiping bystanders, each telling their own version of what happened. "It was a gas leak." "The IRA did it." "It was an earthquake."

Through the throngs of reporters, with flashing box brownies and police taking statements, Gerry noticed the weasel-looking woman he had encountered earlier.

"That's him. He – he went up before the bomb went off!" she shrieked, pointing toward Gerry; this time her directions were for the fresh out of college policeman's attention.

"Stop, in the name of the law," the policeman shouted.

A natural instinct to flee took over and Gerry ran, the light from a flash blinding him. He barged through the crowds, leaving cries of disapproval and police whistles behind. Innocent until proven guilty, he thought, as he darted down a side alley and stepped into a doorway, out of sight. He could have stayed and told his side of events, even proved his innocence but Gerry had more pressing things to do. He had to get to Germany.

* * *

"Oh, how simply awful. They say a Scottish man did it. A MacNeil, I believe."

"No, no, my dear. You couldn't be further from the truth. My mistress just told me. The master, he works for the Evening Standard, don't you know? Well he said that......."

Georgie couldn't help but overhear as the two nannies, dressed as twins, and pushing identical prams, passed him by.

"Excuse me, ladies," he said, interrupting their gossip. "But can I ask what on earth has happened?"

"Have you not heard, sir? There was a......," the first one replied.

"It was a bomb, sir. Killed hundreds, my mistress says," the second one continued. "You can read about it, sir, in the Standard. The master works there, sir, so he does."

Georgie thanked the nannies and left them gossiping, as he crossed the road to the car. Placing a briefcase full of money on the passenger side floor, he noticed Gerry's passport, with the photo of Eloise poking from its folds and, picking it up, he placed it safely in his pocket and started the engine. As he headed out of the city and back to Kelsey Hall, Georgie thought about Gerry. Did he survive the blast and, if he did, was he now a fugitive, with little money and no passport?

"Good luck, old man," he said.

CHAPTER FIFTEEN

Monday 8th October, 6.00 pm

Imagination getting the better of him, Gerry instantly felt fingers pointing and eyes piercing, as he read the headline and studied the wanted photo in the newspaper.

BOMB KILLS

This man, Gerry MacNeil, is suspected of causing an explosion in W2 today. If seen, do not approach, as he may be armed.

Contact Scotland Yard immediately.

He looked from beneath the tattered trilby and pulled the collar of his recently-acquired trench coat up around his face. Not one person was paying attention to the dishevelled-looking man, sat at the back of the smoky workmen's café. But still, Gerry bowed his head.

He sipped from the blue and white enamel cup, savouring the hot, sweet tea and continued to leaf through the paper. Gerry had read all he needed to know; he wasn't interested in any other story. His thoughts were on what to do next and, as he turned the page, an advert caught his eye.

A TIME FOR ADVENTURE

THE GYPSY MOTH

TEACHING THE WORLD TO FLY.

Guaranteed superior all-round performance to that of any machine of the same class in the world.

Ready to fly away.

THE DE HAVILLAND AIRCRAFT COMPANY, LTD

STAG LANE AERODROME – EDGEWARE – MIDDX.

CHAPTER SIXTEEN

Tuesday 9th October, 7:15 am

A four-hour walk and barely six hours of sleep later, Gerry's dreams of Eloise were disturbed. A cockerel sang its early morning crow, sitting proud on a gatepost outside the barn which Gerry had used as dry quarters the previous night. The wet walk through London to the suburbs may not have taken quite as long, had any passing vehicle stopped to give the tramp-like man a lift. Rubbing his eyes, Gerry sat up from beneath the hay. He stretched his aching limbs and stared out at the row of Gypsy Moths in the neighbouring field, they too basking in the sun's warming rays as they broke the horizon.

It was an hour before he left the barn. Now free of the trench coat and trilby and looking half respectable, Gerry made his way to the aerodrome. As he neared the planes, Gerry spotted a young woman, aged about twenty-five and in full flight gear. She was walking around one particular plane, marked GAAA-H, giving it a thorough examination.

"Is it yours?" he asked.

She looked up over the tail, surprised.

"It?" she questioned.

"The plane," Gerry said, "Is it yours?"

"It, sir, will be a he, once I buy him. He's a beauty, isn't he?" she answered, running her hand lovingly over the plane's wing, as she approached him.

"Yes it……he is," Gerry said, correcting himself. "I'm Jason – Jason Ponsonby," he lied.

She held out her hand.

"Amy Johnson."

Amy turned from Gerry. She ran her hand over his - that is - the plane's, sleek fuselage.

"Are you flying or buying?" she asked.

"Hopefully flying but I have a small dilemma."

"Oh?" she replied.

* * *

The 'Artificer', a 386 ton coastal collier, set sail from Dover that same morning. Georgie stood on its stern, looking back at England and the white cliffs, thankful the weather had turned. He didn't think the previous night's rain was ever going to stop and it could have made for a turbulent crossing to Calais. Having not heard from Gerry, he and Archie had loaded the kissel with the essentials. Luggage, fifty thousand pounds and an assortment of weapons. Just the essentials.

* * *

As they sat in the back of the brand new 1928 Duesenberg Model J, Eloise was glad of the violin case that separated her from the slim American. Unable to truly appreciate the beauty of the Black Forest, she stared out at the passing scenery as the car crossed the border into Germany.

"Where's Capone now?" David asked, turning and addressing Spats.

Eloise squirmed; just the sound of his voice made her feel sick.

"Back in the States, Florida. He's just bought a place there," Spats replied.

"Which will soon belong to the Reich," David said. "And his empire will be mine." He rubbed his hands together at the idea.

"Let's get to Friedrichshafen and get what's coming to us," he said.

"I'm sure you will", Eloise muttered under her breath.

The large henchman accelerated and the sleek black car sped on through the forest.

* * *

"What bomb?" Capone asked.

"The one that killed the woman I love," Peter said

Capone held the receiver to his ear, listening.

"If you had anything to do with this, I'll……."

"Listen up, Dann. That hit weren't mine, we wouldn't be speaking if it was," Capone interrupted.

"Your man did it, Capone. He was seen. Where is he? Where's Spatelli? Is he with Steinberg, collecting the fifty grand ransom?"

Al Capone didn't answer.

"Steinberg, you good for nothing, double-crossing rat," he screamed, hurling the telephone through the air. The wires snapped, cutting Peter off in an instant, as it shattered the window in Capone's new home.

"Fifty G is it," Capone screamed. "I'll give you fifty G, Steinberg. It'll be waiting in your grave.

CHAPTER SEVENTEEN

Tuesday 9th October, 8.00 am

"Well, that's my story. I love Eloise and need to get her back," he said.

Having finished tinkering with an aircraft engine, Amy wiped her oily hands on a newspaper and looked at Gerry.

"And you don't have a plane?"

"Huhu."

"And you can't fly?"

Gerry thought back to all the hours he had amassed in the air. He had flown jumbo jets, Lear jets, Cessnas amongst others. But that was in 1994 and on a flight simulator.

"Nope," he replied.

Amy liked him; he had kind eyes and a trusting face. She took one last look at his wanted photo in the Standard, before screwing it up and dropping it in a wastepaper bin.

"Well, you're a knight in shining armour," she said, "and your stallion awaits."

Gerry thanked her and, within minutes of leaving the hangar, they were airborne and on their way to Germany.

CHAPTER EIGHTEEN

Thursday 11th October, 7:15 am

Two days later in Friedrichshafen, the sun was rising just above the horizon and the four of them stood amongst hundreds, all in awe at the gigantic helium-filled airship. Its gondola, a ninety-eight feet flat-bottomed boat housing the control room and passenger areas, hovered just feet above the ground. The D-LZ127 Graf Zeppelin was tethered firmly in place, as the crew made ready for its departure, checking the engines and stowing luggage, which included a small crate marked 'car parts'.

You must be here somewhere, Gerry thought, as he scanned the crowds for Eloise and that bastard, Steinberg. But they were nowhere in sight.

"Good luck, sir," he heard Archie say to Georgie. "I'll be awaiting your safe return home."

"And good luck to you too, Gerry," Amy added.

Gerry looked at her, taken aback at her comment. "You – you know who I am?"

Amy smiled and kissed him on the cheek. "Go rescue your damsel, Gerry MacNeil," she whispered. "Would you like a lift back, Archie?" Amy asked.

"Very kind of you, miss," he replied, "but I must decline. I need to get the car back and I like to keep my feet firmly on the ground."

Which wasn't entirely true….. for a time traveller.

* * *

Having said their goodbyes, Gerry and Georgie boarded the gondola and a young, uniformed, crew member, who introduced himself as Clarence, asked for their passports and tickets.

"Ah yes," Georgie said, remembering he still had Gerry's passport. "I found this back in London."

Gerry thanked him and handed his passport to Clarence.

"I thought you might like this, too," Georgie added. Smiling he handed Gerry a photo of Eloise. Not the one with writing on the back but one that showed her happy and smiling, sat outside the timber-framed orangery. "I thought this one would be much better," he said. Gerry thanked him and studied the photo. He knew he must save her.

Taking their tickets, Clarence smiled as well and offered to show them to their cabin.

"Follow me, gentlemen," he said, leading the way.

They turned left across the dining room and down a corridor, which was flanked either side with cabin doors. Gerry looked in on the ones that were open, hoping he might spot Eloise but, deep down, he knew David wouldn't be that stupid. He would have her locked away, out of sight, until he was ready to make his presence known.

"Here we are, gentlemen," Clarence said, standing to one side so they could enter. He waited with his hand outstretched.

"Ah, yes, of course," Georgie said.

"Thank you, sir. I was asked to give you this," he said, exchanging the tip for a sealed envelope. "If you need anything, anything at all, just ask," he added.

Georgie thanked him and took the envelope. He shut the cabin door and joined Gerry inside.

It was a compact room, decorated with floral wallpaper and containing nothing more than a sofa, which could be converted to an upper and lower berth, a single bedside table and a small window. Georgie sat on the sofa and, placing the case full of money on the floor between his legs, he opened the envelope and read the letter out loud.

"At midday, three days from now, go to the cargo hold with the money. Don't do anything until then, or she'll end up in the drink."

"So what now?" he asked.

Gerry stood looking from the window, thinking. The cheering crowd below continued to wave both German and American flags as the Zeppelin lifted higher, until they completely disappeared from view beneath the low-lying clouds. He turned and faced Georgie.

"Now," he said, "we wait, we plan and we take Clarence up on his offer.

CHAPTER NINETEEN

Saturday 13th October, Midday

During the course of the next few days, Gerry and Georgie had come to befriend Clarence; particularly Gerry, who shared Clarence's enthusiasm for adventure. Hailing from St. Louis in Missouri, the nineteen-year-old golf caddy spent most of his teenage years travelling America as a stowaway, boarding trains and ships along the way, was now on the Zeppelin and, after being discovered, was earning his passage as a cabin boy. Luckily for Gerry and Georgie, he could gain access to areas that they couldn't. He had retrieved their crate of guns, got them uniforms and the three of them had spent many hours studying plans of the airship's layout.

* * *

The wind and rain buffeted hard against the outer skin of the Zeppelin as Gerry, disguised as an engineer and carrying a toolbox containing nothing more than his Browning, entered the map room. An assortment of crew members studying charts were oblivious to his presence, as he crossed the room and made for a ladder leading to the ship's hull. A radio crackled to life in the room next door.

"Delta Lima Zulu 127, please confirm you are passing through a mid-ocean weather front."

"Roger Delta Lima Zulu, out," the radio operator replied.

Distracted by the weather, no-one questioned his agenda, as Gerry climbed the ladder into the hull and along the keel corridor.

The hull was immense and full of duralumin girders crisscrossing the entire length of the structure in a triangular construction. Gerry headed along the corridor, beneath the massive canisters of Blau Gas, past the crew quarters and finally into the cargo hold.

Above him in the axial corridor, Georgie waited, out of sight but with a clear view of the hold. His grip tightened on the rifle as David came into view, leading Eloise before him at gunpoint.

"No further, MacNeil," David warned, shouting over the sound of the weather.

Gerry stopped and grabbed a girder with his free hand, steadying himself as the airship lurched sideways in the wind. "Are you okay, Els?" he asked.

Eloise nodded. "I'm fine," she said, her smile telling Gerry that her spirits were still high.

"How touching," David interrupted. "Love's young dream. Now MacNeil, where's my money?"

"It's here," Gerry replied, holding up the toolbox.

"And where's the other one?" David asked.

"The other one?" Gerry questioned.

"Ponsonby, of course. Surely he didn't send a boy to do a man's job."

Gerry studied him, ignoring the comment. "What is it you're really up to, Stienberg?" he demanded.

Before David could reply, Eloise interrupted. "He's more a man than you could ever be, you cad."

David grabbed Eloise around the waist and stroked her cheek with his Walther gun. "Now, now, that's no way for a lady to behave," he said. Eloise stopped her struggle, as he pressed the barrel of his gun to her temple.

"What am I up to? Ah! Now there's a question, MacNeil," David replied. "It's all for the good of the fatherland, you see. As we both know, Winston Churchill will become prime minister and bring about the end of the war but, by eliminating him now before that happens, there will be no stopping the power of the Reich and our takeover of the world, including your puny English island."

"So where does Capone fit in?" Gerry asked.

"My scapegoat. With Spatelli killing Churchill, Capone gets the blame and I take over his empire."

"You'll never get away with it."

"But I will, Gerry. Miss Love was more loyal to me than she made out. It's amazing the things that get divulged between the sheets." He pulled Eloise closer and stroked her cheek with his Walther. "As I'm sure you were hoping to find out for yourself. Isn't that right, Els?"

"Get away from me, you dirty scum," she said.

"What did she tell you?" Gerry asked.

"What?"

"Miranda. What did she tell you?"

"Other than that she would do anything for me, you mean? Silly girl. Well, it also seems that Mr. Churchill will be in............"

* * *

"Full ahead," Captain Eckener said.

Clarence stood silent in the doorway. He looked out past the control panel at the strengthening weather as the captain gave his orders, sending the ship deeper into the squall.

"Steady as she goes," Eckener added.

The rain lashed hard against the control room windows, driven on by the prevailing winds. With the visibility near to zero, an inexperienced crewman grasped the elevator wheel, trying his hardest to keep control.

"Keep it steady, son," Eckener said, moving forward next to the young crewman.

"Aye, sir," the crewman replied, nervously.

Without warning, and with no time to react, the nose of the airship was forced upwards, rising high above the horizon. Loose objects flew in Clarence's direction, as he gripped the doorframe, saving himself from falling backwards.

The captain instantly grabbed the wheel, struggling to gain control. Gradually, the nose lowered bit by bit, until the horizon once more came into view beneath the cloud base. A silence befell the control room, broken only by the tinned mechanical voice from the communications tube.

"Sir, we have a tear in the port fin," it announced.

* * *

Everything seemed to slow down, as if time itself had stopped. With his hand still gripping the girder, Gerry's body span, the momentum forcing the tool box to release and fly through the air in David and Eloise's direction. They too began to topple and Eloise's arms were flailing in the air, desperately seeking something to hold on to. With the whole of her weight against him, David instinctively released his hold. His gun-toting hand banged hard against a girder, sending the Walther to the depths of the balloon. The toolbox, narrowly missing Eloise, connected squarely with

David's head as he fell. He was motionless, unconscious, his body softening Eloise's own fall.

Meanwhile, in the axial corridor, Georgie involuntarily rolled forward, causing his finger to tighten around the trigger of the rifle. With an explosion, the bullet erupted from the barrel and flew the length of the ship's hull, through the airship's outer skin and ripped into the port fin, tearing it in two.

* * *

As Captain Eckener brought the Graf Zeppelin to a halt some two hundred feet above the choppy Atlantic Ocean, Gerry helped Eloise to her feet and cradled her in his arms. She buried her head into his chest, relieved to be safe in his embrace once again.

"Well," Gerry said, "that's the second time since meeting him that I've knocked him off his feet." He eyed the unconscious Stienberg.

"But what do we do with him?" Georgie asked, as he descended a ladder to join them.

"Daddy!" Eloise shrieked. "You're here!"

"Of course, my dear. No one kidnaps my family and gets away with it."

"My heroes," she said.

As two heroes and one damsel stood arm-in-arm pondering over David, Clarence joined them. "You can put him in my quarters, until we reach land," he offered.

* * *

Gerry trained his gun on their captor, as Georgie gagged and bound him to the bunk. Having been introduced to Eloise, Clarence had since left and was now helping other crew members repair the damaged fin.

"Can't we just throw him overboard?" Eloise asked.

"Maybe later Els, but not until he gives us more information," Gerry said, bluffing.

"Besides," Georgie said, looking back and giving them both a wink, "I think Capone may have his own plans for our good friend, Mr. Stienberg, here."

The fear in David's eyes showed as he heard their words, but his own muffled cries of protest fell on deaf ears. He knew only too well what would befall him in the hands of Capone; that thought made being dropped in the Atlantic seem much more appealing for, at least then, he wouldn't have concrete shoes weighing him down.

CHAPTER TWENTY

Monday 15th October, Dusk

After successfully making it through a second squall off the coast of Bermuda, the Zeppelin moored safely with the mast at Lakehurst, New Jersey. With the help of Clarence, Georgie was able to send a telegram home and had arranged transportation on their arrival; so now, Gerry, Georgie and Eloise wheeled a man-sized, unmarked crate away under the shadow of darkness to a nearby hangar, whilst the remaining passengers and crew received a heroes' welcome and a ticker-tape parade along New York City's Broadway.

"Welcome to America, Stienberg," Gerry said to the crate. "Nothing like a bit of first class travel, is there?"

The crate rocked, nearly toppling, as the irate passenger struggled within, cursing in a muffled German dialect.

"Where shall we take him?" Gerry asked.

"Chicago," Georgie replied. "I have a warehouse in the North Side; we can go there while we decide what to do."

* * *

When they reached the hangar, Georgie went to look for the transport, leaving Gerry and Eloise alone. They perched atop of the crate, without a care for the comfort of its contents and Eloise leaned into Gerry, as he removed his jacket and placed it over her shoulders.

"Thank you, Bumble," she said.

"I've not heard that in a while," he smiled.

"Oh, Gerry, you'll always be my Bumble, no matter what happens."

"And so much has happened," he replied, "but I would imagine there's more yet to come."

Eloise leaned closer into him as Gerry planted a kiss on the top of her head, savouring the softness of her hair that felt smooth to his lips.

"Then we will do it together," she said.

They sat silent for a moment, both deep in their own thoughts when, suddenly, they were bathed in headlights, as the sound of a Fargo truck drawing closer filled the air.

"Gerry, open the back, could you, old bean?" Georgie said from the driver's side window, as he pulled up alongside them.

Gerry jumped from the crate, giving it a bang as he did so.

"Wakey wakey, David," he said. "Time to go, as your old friend's looking forward to seeing you.

CHAPTER TWENTY-ONE

Tuesday 16th October, Time Unknown

David could feel every turn, every stop, every pothole.

"Every damn pothole," he said.

He had no idea how much time had passed since he was hoisted into the back of the vehicle, but long enough and, with a little brute force, it allowed him to loosen the lid of his makeshift prison.

Thankfully, but mistakenly, his captors had released him from his bonds, before nailing the lid shut. Big mistake.

Another pothole, only this time it was deeper and the timing was perfect. As he placed his hands against the lid, his body lifted with a thump, forcing the lid to loosen completely.

* * *

Eloise stirred, but didn't wake, as Gerry drove over another pothole. She snuggled against her father's chest, exhausted.

"Ssshh now," Georgie whispered, as he brushed hair from her cheek. It had been a long time since he had held her like that and memories of tucking her in and bedtime stories began to fill his mind. Now she was all grown up and a beautiful young lady, just like her mother before her.

"She's going to be heartbroken, Gerry," Georgie said silently. "When you leave, I mean."

"I know. Me too."

Gerry stared ahead, watching the road as the headlights cut through the darkened road before them.

"I may not go back, Georgie," he said. "What if I don't accomplish it? Whatever it is. What then?"

"That I don't know, my dear fellow but one has to try, don't you think?" Georgie replied.

He looked down at his daughter, looking so vulnerable as she slept. "Who knows who may suffer, if we don't?" he added.

"Of course, you're right," Gerry said. "The sooner we have a proper talk with Steinberg the better, at least then we'll know what we…….."

"Look out!!" Georgie hollered.

It was too late; the large pothole caught the left front wheel before Gerry had a chance to steer from its path. With the bang and thud, thud, thud that followed, it was obvious to them both that a tyre had punctured. Gerry depressed the accelerator, slowing the truck so as not to cause further damage, before finally braking to a halt.

"What happened?" Eloise asked, rubbing her eyes and stretching awake.

"We've got a flat," Gerry replied, as he climbed from the van.

"A flat?" Eloise yawned.

"A puncture. We hit a hole," Gerry said. "It's nothing to worry about. You stay here and your father and I will have a look."

Gerry closed the door behind him and was soon joined by Georgie, as he prodded the tyre with his foot.

"Yup, defo flat." he said.

Georgie also prodded the wheel, as if he too was confirming it was flat.

"Indeed it is. We passed a petrol station a few miles back," he said. "I can walk back and get help."

"Sounds like a good idea but shouldn't we check on Mister in the back first, though?" Gerry asked.

"Damned if you're not wrong, Gerry MacNeil. Damned if you're not."

* * *

David stayed silent and crouched beside the now empty crate, as he listened to the conversation from outside the van. He smiled to himself, knowing that surprise would be on his side but, still, he would have to act quickly. Wishing for his gun, David felt around in the darkness for a weapon, anything that would give him the upper hand and a chance to pummel that 'Fettbacke', MacNeil.

"Yup, defo flat," he heard MacNeil say. How he hated the British accent, especially his, Gerry bloody MacNeil's, with its common twang and twenty-first century shortcuts. "If only I could knock those out of him," he said to himself.

David swept his hand across the floor before him and found what he was looking for. His grip tightened around the crowbar as he picked it up, testing its weight and slamming it into the palm of his free hand.

While he waited in the dark, David listened to the footsteps of his enemies as they made their way to the back of the van. "Damned if you're not" was spoken before he heard the handle of the door release from its lock. Like a caged lion escaping from its confines, David sprang. He barged into the opening door, sending Georgie flying backwards onto the road and, before Gerry had a chance to slam the adjoining door closed, David was out. He was free. As he leapt from the van, the crowbar swung in an arc, narrowly missing Gerry's shoulder before its claw embedded into the van's wooden panelling. It held fast as David landed, expertly and squarely, on his feet. With years of Nazi training behind him, he rolled forward, was up again in no time and fled into the woods, leaving his stunned captors staring in his wake.

* * *

The solitary light flickered with life, teasing the moths that danced around its element, the movement of their rapidly flapping wings causing particles of dust to fall from the sign that hung above the door. MEL's Garage and Diner, it read.

The man in the dirt-encrusted suit cupped his hands against the glass and peered into the darkness beyond. He grabbed the handle and the door rattled on its hinges, as he forced it with his shoulder, and another sign spun from 'Closed' to 'Open' as the door flew inwards, "Veradammt," he said, falling in after it.

Once he found his footing, he made his way behind the counter. Picking up some Hershy bars, he filled his pockets before dialling the phone.

"Mr. Capone," he said, with a mouth full of nougat, "it's David. David Steinberg."

CHAPTER TWENTY-TWO

Wednesday 17th October, 8:25 am

His head was pounding; it was like he had been hit with a golf ball. In fact, a dozen golf balls, yet there was no pretty young lady to dress his wound this time.

"So you's the infamous Gerry MacNeil I keeps hearing all about."

Puffing on a large Cuban cigar, a bulk of a man loomed over Gerry, looking down at him as he rubbed his head, whilst he sat, squatting against the van. The pot-bellied henchman standing next to Al Capone seemed small in comparison; he nursed the butt of his tommy gun, just to make sure Gerry's head hadn't damaged it, as Capone continued.

"Seems likes yous been a bad boy, Gerry," he said "Beens sticking ya nose in wheres it's not wanted, right?"

"Just looking after the things I care about, Capone," Gerry replied.

"Aaawww, how touching. He cares. Now ain't that touching, Mr. Capone?" the henchman said.

"Well it's gotta stop, see," Capone continued, ignoring him. "Now on your feet."

Gerry grabbed hold of the van and pulled himself up. Once steady, he looked around for signs of Eloise and her father but they were nowhere to be seen. The last time he saw them was when they arrived at the North Side warehouse. Gerry had left the van and started to open the large, green wooden doors of the building, when he was hit from behind. That was the last thing he remembered.

"Where's Els and Georgie?" he asked.

"The Ponsonbys?" Capone said, "Yous see them soon enough but, first, let's talk about the money."

"The money?" Gerry asked, knowing full well what Capone meant.

"The fifty G, you schmuck."

"Oh, *that* money. Well, I got the girl back, didn't I?" Gerry said, poker-faced.

"Don't yous be gettin' smart whit me, MacNeil."

"You wants me to give him what's for, boss?" the henchman added, pointing his gun at Gerry.

"You'll get your money, Capone. Surely Steinberg told you he has it," Gerry said, standing his ground. He waited, watching Capone's reaction before continuing.

"Ah, I see. He didn't, did he?" Gerry smiled. "You just don't know who you can trust these days, do you, Capone."

"Indeed he doesn't, Gerry, my old friend."

Peter Dann laid his silver-topped cane on the henchman's gun, gesturing him to lower it, as he pushed his silenced Walther into the small of Al Capone's back.

Like a silent invader, Peter had moved with stealth, as he entered the warehouse just moments earlier.

"Dann!!" Capone said. "How's the hell did you……..."

"Don't you worry about that, Capone. Now let's go and get the Ponsonbys and talk about your options."

* * *

"So there you have it," Gerry said. "Steinberg plans to take you down. You're to get the blame for Churchill's assassination, he gets to enjoy your empire and, all the while, you'll be watching from behind bars in Alcatraz, or worse."

Capone let out a deep, rolling laugh that echoed throughout Peter's hotel room.

The four of them, reunited once more, looked on, wondering why he found it so funny.

"Alcatraz? You Limeys have no idea, do yous?." he said, still laughing. "No-one, even yous, Dann, will ever have enough to pin on me."

"Ness does," Peter said coolly.

Capone paled and a look of fear washed over him. An instant silence befell the room, a silence that was almost as deafening as Capone's own bellowing.

"Ness?" Georgie and Eloise questioned together. "What's ness?"

"An untouchable," Peter said. "Elliot Ness, a most feared adversary, isn't that right, Al?"

Without giving Capone time to answer, Peter continued.

"What you don't realise Capone, is that Ness does in fact have enough evidence to send you to the chair but this is where you and I can help each other," he continued. "You find out what Steinberg knows and I guarantee your life."

"And Alcatraz?" Capone asked.

"Oh, you'll definitely be spending a little time there, my friend," Peter said. "Maybe for a few tax issues, which will at least save you from the chair."

"And once I give yous what yous wants, what happens to Steinberg?" Capone asked.

"Do with him what you will," Peter replied.

"It was meant to be," Gerry whispered to Georgie.

* * *

After their little soirée, Capone left with his henchman, leaving the four would-be adventurers raising a glass to their success.

"Here's to the future," Peter said.

"To our future," Eloise said, grabbing and squeezing Gerry's hand, "and I think this has something to do with it."

The three men looked on, as Eloise dug into her riding boot.

"I found this when David held me captive," she explained, producing a paper scroll. "I had instructions to give it directly to you, Peter."

Peter took the ageing scroll and unravelled it, taking a moment to read its contents to himself.

"Good old George," he laughed.

"Excuse me?" Georgie said.

"Not you, Daddy," Eloise said, "It's from Grandpapa."

"Indeed it is," Peter said. "Indeed it is."

He proceeded to read out the scroll to the intrigued trio.

'Take your cane, unscrew the top,

The key inside, will undo the lock,

310 South Central, On All Hallows' Eve,

And history will repeat itself, I so believe.'

"Oh, how awfully exciting. Another riddle," Eloise said.

"Another, Els?" Gerry asked.

"Yes, from Grandpapa George, along with this note."

Eloise produced another piece of paper and this time read it out loud herself.

To my darling granddaughter, Eloise,

At first you may find this hard to believe, but believe you must.

I travelled a great distance, and over many years, to write this, as I once was asked to by a fellow traveller and a good friend of your father's and Gerry's, a professor Clarence Teoli.

"Who?" Gerry asked, interrupting Eloise. "Clarence?"

"Wait," Peter insisted. "Let her finish."

Eloise took a long sip of Earl Grey tea and continued.

'We spent many a day together at Rose Cottage in his later years, talking about his past but, as his days neared to an end, he told me he had a secret he needed to share. A secret he had kept for many years. He asked that I pass this message on to you.

Gerry, my friend, I so enjoyed getting to know you and sharing with you our own tales of adventure on the Zeppelin. Of course, the one that interested me most was how the numbers three and ten were linked to you being in 1928 and of your life in 1994 here at Rose Cottage, where I now convalesce.

Georgie, I thank you for your generous gift of £10,000 that set me on my way to a life of study, thus allowing me to master the art of time travel and send young George back to 1864 to purchase Kelsey Hall and get this message to you.

A TIME FOR ADVENTURE

Peter Dann, you old coot, I thank you for giving me a place to rest my ageing bones and I trust you have taken care of the cane entrusted to you.

Eloise, on October 16th 1928, in a Chicago hotel, you must give the scroll that accompanies this letter to Peter.

Your eternal friend, Clarence.

Now my darling Eloise, stow these notes on your person and keep them safe until the four of you reunite in Chicago. The world as you will know it depends on you all.

Your ever loving granddad,

George.

P.S. It was meant to be!!"

Peter, who had a feeling that this moment would eventually come, rested his bearded chin on his cane, the same cane that Granddad George had bequeathed to him on his passing, requesting in his will that he guard it closely.

Georgie, taking stock of the situation, sat mouth agape as it all sunk in, still unsure what to make of all the time travelling stuff. Gerry, on the other hand, had questions to ask.

"So our good friend Clarence was able to send him here all those years ago to get this message to us and kept it a secret to his dying days?"

"Apparently so," Eloise replied. "Oh, this really is very exciting," she added.

"It's amazing," Gerry said.

As they all sat contemplating the complexities of it all, Georgie finally added his own thoughts.

"I have to say, old beans," he said, "I am ever so slightly confused."

This made the other three break away from the seriousness of the events for a moment and together they all broke into laughter.

"You and me both," Gerry laughed. "You and me both."

"Well, then," Peter said, as he unscrewed the silver top from the cane, "let's see if this key and what Capone finds out hold the answers.

CHAPTER TWENTY-THREE

Wednesday 17th October, 1:55 pm

"Tell me what you knows, schmuck."

"I'm telling ya, I don't know any……."

The large man took one last gulp of air before the freezing water of the Chicago river covered his frame. For the third time, he was submerged beneath its ice-covered surface.

Struggling was of no use; the ropes that bound his hands and feet had started to cut into his skin and he could taste the blood as it began to cloud the water. If hyperthermia or sharks didn't kill him, Capone's henchman surely would. Either way, he knew his time was up.

As bubbles of air escaped his burning lungs, he felt his life flash before him, his youth, his marriage, his children and, of course, the things he had done whilst driving for David Steinberg. Those awful, horrific, things.

Suddenly and with force, his head broke the surface, bringing him back from his memories.

"Last chance, schmuck," he heard the henchman say.

A TIME FOR ADVENTURE

The large man gasped for air, taking deep gulps before he could reply.

"Oookkkkaaaay," he shivered. "I'll tell you everything."

* * *

If it wasn't for the broken clumps of ice that floated along below them as they stood on the hotel's balcony overlooking the Chicago river, it could have been mistaken for a summer's day. The sun beamed from a cloudless blue sky and warmed them, as Eloise smiled widely at Gerry.

"So you really are a time traveller, Bumble," she said.

"Well, yes, now you come to mention it," he replied, smiling. "I suppose I am."

"I always knew there was something special about you, Bumble."

"Me?" he replied. "What about you Els, with all that you've been though? Yet you're still smiling. You really are a special lady."

"I had you with me all the way and that's what really kept me going," she said. "And now we can grow old together."

Gerry stared down at the passing river, biting his lower lip, seeming to drift off into a world of his own for a moment or two.

"Bumble?"

Broken from his thoughts, Gerry looked to Eloise.

"There's something you should know, Els," he said. "About my future here, in this time, something Peter told me to be prepared for and it's only fair you prepare too. He told me that I can't stay in this time forever."

"Gerry, now you're scaring me. What do you mean?"

"I'll leave this time Els. Once I've dealt with David and his wretched plan, I'll simply disappear."

"Oh, Bumble. No. Please, there must be something we can do?"

Burying herself into Gerry, Eloise, rested her head on his shoulder. She didn't want to let him go, not now she had found him. As she held him tight in her arms, a solitary drop escaped her tearful eyes.

There must be a way, Gerry thought, as Eloise sobbed silently. Someone must know the answer. Someone must be in control.

As two lovers, who had found each other through extraordinary circumstances stood on a balcony, a single, salty droplet of water fell into the river below, where in its depths a large German man swayed in its flow, secured in his watery grave by a chain and a large concrete block.

* * *

As he raised the scope to his eye, his breathing steadied with each outward breath, sending a trail of vapour into the warm afternoon sky. He knelt, resting the barrel of his Springfield M1903 sniper rifle between the swirls of the balcony's ornate iron railings. He smiled to himself, as the man and woman appeared from the hotel room across the river, laughing with each other, seeming so happy. So in love.

For two hours he had waited for this moment, to see them together. Now, finally, he could kill two birds with one stone. Squinting against the sun, he adjusted the rifle's telescopic sight, until his view focussed on the pair. His finger rested next to the trigger, not quite on it but waiting, ready for the right moment to strike.

He watched as the woman held the man and, even from where he was standing, he could see the sadness in her eyes, as she rested her head on his shoulder. She blinked and appeared to stare directly at him. Now. It had to be now.

There it was, at last; it was only for an instant but enough to get his attention. The sunlight reflected from another telescopic sight also trained on Eloise and Gerry. He swung his barrel to the left, until he had Spatelli in his sights. Taking a breath as his fingers touched the trigger, he squeezed gently and, with a crack, the stock recoiled into his shoulder as the .30 caliber projectile left the muzzle and homed in on its target.

It struck; the bullet ripped through Spatelli's forearm, forcing him to release his grip as bone, cartilage and blood exited the wound left behind from the impact.

"First bird taken care of," Clarence said to himself, "and the second one's safe."

CHAPTER TWENTY-FOUR

Wednesday 17th October, 5.20 pm

The snow was starting to fall, as Peter leant against the bonnet of Al Capone's green and black 1928 Cadillac V-8 Sedan and watched as the homeless and destitute souls of Chicago stood in line, coughing deep chesty coughs, or scratching lice that had made homes in their matted hair and scraggly beards, each eager to enjoy a hot meal from one of the many soup kitchens Al Capone had set up. He couldn't help but have pity for them, especially as they faced this time of year both alone and cold on the streets.

"That's one part about you I admire, Capone," Peter said.

"This," Capone replied, spreading his arms out to the queue, "it's in my blood, see. Times was tough, even for me once, too. I'm giving something back, see."

Even though their paths had crossed on many fraught occasions over the years, Peter held a touch of respect for what Capone did here but not enough to gain his trust completely.

"So tell me about Steinberg," he said. "What did your man find out?"

A TIME FOR ADVENTURE

Capone brushed away the flakes of snow that had settled on his fur-lined collar, before pulling it up around his neck and then took a long, hard draw on his cigar, before answering.

"Wells, for one," he said, "I knows that's he's a good for nothing, double-crossing, schmuck, that will soon be joining his fat friend."

"And Churchill?" Peter asked.

"Hey, yous!" Capone shouted, addressing a vagrant that had foolhardily jumped the queue.

Suddenly, the line went quiet as the others stepped back, leaving the foolish man to fall to his knees. Raising his hands to his lips and clenching them together, he looked up at Capone.

"Mr. Capone," he said, pleading. "Please, Mr. Capone."

"Mario, teach this schmuck a lesson."

"Ah boss, but he stinks."

Without the need to say anything, Capone shot the young gangster a look that said 'do it now, or else.'

The rookie, who should have known better, immediately raced over and kicked the vagrant full force in the stomach, sending him flying backwards. With a thud, the bedraggled man hit the ground in a lifeless manner.

"Next time," he said, "you do as Mr. Capone says, get me, you dirty guttersnipe!"

As he stood over the helpless man, the rookie turned to Capone smiling, waiting further instructions.

His boss nodded a single nod.

That was all that was needed. The rookie kicked the man once more for good measure. The sound of his jaw cracking reverberated around the soup kitchen's courtyard and the snow beneath his head turned a deep blood red.

"Yep, that's the other side of the Alphonse Capone I know," Peter said.

"Churchill," Capone continued, as if nothing but the normal had happened, "he's gonna be attending a Halloween ball at the Coliseum on the thirty first and that's where Steinberg's gonna takes him out."

"How Capone? How?"

"The fat man didn't knows, he would have spilled the beans if he did. My boys made sure of that, see," Capone insisted.

* * *

David stood and watched as the terrified vet, more used to dealing with horses than gangsters, went to work on Spatelli's wounded arm. The man couldn't help but shake, as he was forced to prepare a sterile dressing, all the while keeping one eye on the silenced Luger that was pointed in his direction.

"Well, did you get him?" David asked Spatelli.

"What! Are you serious?" he replied angrily.

Ripping his bloodied arm from the grip of the vet, he held it up for David to see.

"Look at this, look what they done to me," he added.

"You'll live," David replied. "Ain't that right, doc, he'll live?"

"H…he was lucky, y…yes, sir, he c….c…..could have severed an artery," the vet stammered.

"Y….y…you call this lucky, old man?" Spatelli mocked, "Now hurry, fix me up."

The vet doused the dressing in more antiseptic than was needed and held it over Spatelli's arm.

"T....this will hurt a little, sir," he lied.

Before his patient had a chance to reply, the vet forced the dressing onto the open wound, and smiled inwardly as Spatelli squealed like a pig being slaughtered.

"Stop your whining, man," David said. "Now, are we ready for the other business?"

Spatelli's eyes focussed on the vet before answering and he gave a stare so cold, that death itself would run and hide. Even without eye contact, the vet could feel it boring into his soul, as he kept his head bowed and continued to wrap the wound.

"Yes, it's done. Everything's almost in place," he said. "I'm going back later for one final check."

"Make sure it is, Spatelli," David ordered. "The Reich are counting on it."

"A...a...all done, sir," the vet said.

David gave him a wry smile then fired a single, silent shot from his Luger. The old man didn't even flinch but simply bent at the waist and, with a clutter of kidney-shaped pans and metal veterinarian utensils, he slumped lifeless across a table, as the bullet entered dead centre into his forehead.

"Y....y...yes, you're all done," Spatelli mocked once again, as both men left the surgery.

CHAPTER TWENTY-FIVE

Saturday 20th October, 11.15 pm

310 South Central wasn't at all what he expected. The large wooden door that stood before him reminded Gerry of Kelsey Hall's own ornate entrance way, except this one hadn't seen years of welcoming visitors across its threshold. Caked with years of rust, the hinge looked like it would hold the door fast and the numbers etched deep into its grain were faded and barely visible. The door itself was built into a castellated wall that formed part of a turret, rising high into the air. Illuminated by the shine of the moon, the words 'COLISEUM' sat arched between a near identical turret, standing like stone bookmarks, holding the letters up and securing them in place.

Why, he thought. Why here? What's so important about the Chicago Coliseum?"

"Well, Gerry, let's see if we can finally get some answers," he said to himself.

Taking the key that had been hidden in Peter's cane for all those years, he slid it into the keyhole and turned it once in an anti-clockwise direction. With a click, the inner mechanisms of the lock started to come alive and the boing of a spring uncoiling, cog grinding against cog and bolts sliding on the inner side of the door all grabbed his attention.

This doesn't seem like any ordinary lock, he thought, but what's been ordinary about any of this? With one further click, the door sprang open, to reveal a dimly-lit stairway. Peering in and finding nothing untoward, Gerry started his assent.

* * *

The room at the top of the stairs was nothing more than a simple circular closet, barely six feet round. Slicing through the darkness, the moonlight filtered through a solitary window that sat ajar in the turret's stone walls. It cut through the dust that had been rising near his footfalls and its rays fell on the only piece of furniture in the room; an old wooden table on which sat a green, leather-bound, book. Taking a few paces forward, Gerry picked up the book and blew the settling dust from its cover, revealing gold guilt lettering in its title, 'A Time for Adventure, by Clarence Teoli."

Holding it to the light, Gerry began to read the handwritten contents out loud.

"October 1928.

First Encounter with Gerry MacNeil.

Gerry told me his story, a story of time travel, a story I had to learn more about......"

Gerry thought back to just a few days earlier, when he and Clarence had met. Smiling to himself, he skipped forward a few pages and continued to read.

"1969

First prototype of the machine is ready. I have yet to think of what to call this contraption but it's all coming together nicely......."

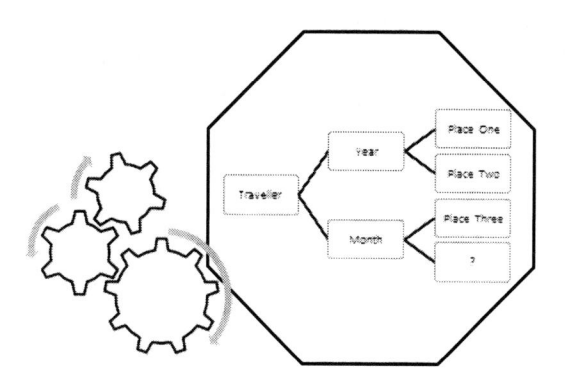

"1984

$Mi(2) = 1-9(C2) =$ *déjà vu*

The Time Controller is finally ready….."

"1994

Now I have the DNA match from his strand of hair, I will be sending a subconscious part of young George back to 1864 to purchase Kelsey Hall and make ready a secret room for the machine."

Gerry read on.

"By now, Gerry, you will have found this journal and know that it is I who lead you to where you are. The chapters are now drawing to a close, as is my lifetime but, Gerry, this is only the beginning for you and your time for adventure. You now have the chance to make the world a better and safer place. It was meant to be."

As he leafed through the remainder of the journal, a tuneful whistle of Yankee Doodle filled the air, drifting in from the open window. Crouching low and keeping to the shadows, he made his way over and peered out. Smelling the staleness of cigarette smoke as it wafted up from the street, and even before seeing his fine Italian clothes and slick black hair, Gerry knew immediately who stood below.

"Spatelli," he whispered. "Now what are you doing here?"

A TIME FOR ADVENTURE

Feeling a rush of adrenalin, Gerry closed and pocketed the journal. Silently, he made his way down the stairs and out into the street but Spatelli was nowhere to be seen. All that remained was a dying cigarette butt and a set of fresh footprints in the snow that disappeared into the coliseum's main entrance.

You're right, Clarence, this certainly is an adventure, Gerry thought, as he followed the prints.

* * *

The interior of the coliseum was immense. Its central arena was bare but for a raised stage that sat to the far end, from where Gerry had entered. Rows of uncomfortable tiered wooden seats surrounded the arena and, above, for those who could afford it, the balcony areas offered softer seating. Gerry looked up to the ceiling that was reminiscent of the zeppelin's own concave, iron-beamed, interior, trying to locate Spatelli, as his whistling resonated around the building.

Gerry ducked from sight as, behind him, the door closed with a squeak, causing the tune to falter. As quickly as it had stopped, the whistling started once again but Gerry could sense a change in its tone, as he crawled on all fours between the chairs.

Reaching the end of an aisle, Gerry paused and listened.

"Come on, show yourself," he muttered.

There was nothing, no clue. The acoustics of the structure made it difficult for Gerry to pinpoint Spatelli's exact location.

Still on his knees, and dodging the discarded bottles left behind by the previous audience, Gerry moved on. Keeping close to the wall which separated seating area A from area B, he edged closer to the central arena. He didn't notice the silence immediately but, by then, it was too late. The plaster from the wall exploded behind him, showering Gerry with fine white powder, as a bullet struck inches from his right shoulder. Instinctively, he fell to the floor and rolled for cover, as another bullet whistled over his head, splintering the back of an aisle chair.

"Get up you, Limey coward!" Spatelli hollered.

Staying quiet and looking beneath the rows, Gerry could see him sitting casually on the edge of the stage, waving his gun in a circular motion, as if conducting an invisible orchestra.

"You got nowhere to go, MacNeil."

Of course, Gerry knew Spatelli was right but he still searched for a way out. Could he make a dash out the way he came in? No, he'd likely get a bullet in the back. Would he make it by leaping over the wall with its six feet drop and trying to limp to the exit? Again, no. As he raised his head to see the options before him, another bullet slammed into the chair.

"Not much of a shot are you, Spatelli?" Gerry shouted.

"You'll see, MacNeil. If it wasn't for this goddamn arm, you'd be dead three times over."

Gerry wondered what he meant by his 'goddamn arm'. Was he injured? Then, as Spatelli leapt from the stage, he saw the bandage that covered Spatelli's sleeveless arm. Could he use this to his advantage? If only he could get a clearer look at his gun then maybe, just maybe.

All Gerry could do now was watch and wait, as Spatelli started to head in his direction.

There it was, just as Gerry suspected, a Smith and Wesson M&P .38 special. The favoured gangster handgun, just like he remembered reading about.

Three shots fired, he thought, and just three to go. Then, remembering the bottles, Gerry reached back with his foot, teasing one gently until it was within arm's length.

"Hey, Spatelli!" he shouted. "Catch!"

Taking the bottle by the neck, Gerry tossed it up and over the seats. He watched as it tumbled through the air like a hand grenade, as Spatelli raised his gun and fired. Missing it completely, the bottle smashed on the ground behind him.

"Fore!" Gerry said, using the golfing term he had used many times before.

With two shots left in the chamber, he knew he needed to act fast, as Spatelli was drawing nearer.

"Why are you here, Spatelli?" he shouted. "Why the coliseum?"

"None of your concern, you just worry about your last minutes here."

Gerry could tell by the volume of his voice that Spatelli was close now and not likely to miss the next shot but he had to take a chance. Springing to his feet, Gerry ran as hard and as fast as he could.

Zigzagging towards the arena, he saw Spatelli with his outstretched arm wavering side to side, trying to take an unsteady aim. Twenty feet, ten feet, five. Gerry dived just as the crack of the gun sounded and the rush of the bullet flew past his ear.

"One!" he screamed involuntarily, crashing into Spatelli. "One bullet left!"

As they fell, the gun slid across the floor, spinning on the polished wooden surface. He crawled forward grasping for it but the gun was just out of reach and Spatelli punched blow upon blow into Gerry's ribcage, making him recoil in pain. Lifting his elbow, Gerry brought it down with force, connecting with Spatelli's cheek, dazing him. The blows stopped momentarily, giving him time to stretch a little further, until he could feel the gun beneath his fingers. With one last push, he grabbed it and, ignoring the heat from the still hot barrel, he held it firmly. Suddenly, he felt a searing pain in his groin, as Spatelli raised a knee, causing Gerry to roll to one side in agony. With no time to react, Spatelli was on him, looking down through evil eyes and, with a distorted smile on his swollen, bloodied lips, he began to crush Gerry's larynx with both hands.

"You're mine now, MacNeil," he said.

Gasping for breath, Gerry grabbed Spatelli's bandaged arm and squeezed hard until the grip around his own neck loosened. Breathing in deeply, Gerry swung the gun, smashing its butt again and again into Spatelli's temple.

Not fazed, Spatelli grabbed at the gun, surprising Gerry on how strong he was for a man of his slim build. They wrestled, each trying desperately to get control when suddenly, with a bang, the last of the bullets erupted from the barrel.

Instantly, Gerry could feel the warmth of the blood soaking through his clothes and, though he felt no pain, the look on Spatelli's face told him what he needed to know.

Tugging Gerry's shirt, Spatelli pulled him close and whispered his dying words.

"Won't….find it…..Limey……"

"Don't you die on me yet," Gerry said, pushing the gangster to one side. "What won't I find? Tell me," he added.

Spats Spatelli spoke no more that night, or ever again.

* * *

"He's dead?" Peter asked.

"Yes, it was either him or me," Gerry replied.

He could see the joy on Peter's face but the look in his eyes showed a different emotion. Regret. Not for the death of Spatelli but for the fact that he hadn't been the one to pull the trigger, in revenge for the murder of Miranda Love.

A TIME FOR ADVENTURE

As Gerry told the story of finding the journal and his encounter with Spatelli, they all listened with interest, with Peter sipping a large whisky, Georgie on the edge of his seat and Eloise tending to Gerry's wounds.

"What did he mean, 'you won't find it'?" she asked. "Find what?"

Gerry winced as Eloise gently dabbed his bruises with iodine.

"I can only imagine a weapon, my dear," Peter replied for Gerry. "Maybe a bomb."

"Oh, gosh! Really?"

"At the coliseum?" Georgie asked.

"Yes and, according to Capone, on the thirty first, at midnight," Peter informed him. "Did you notice anything, Gerry?" he asked.

"No, I didn't hang around. Once I heard the sirens approaching, I got out as quickly as I could."

"Well, the police will be crawling all over the place by now," Peter said.

"So what do we do?" Gerry asked.

"There's only one thing we can do," Peter replied.

"What?" the other three asked in unison.

"Get the hell out of here."

"What about Steinberg?" Georgie asked.

"He's Capone's problem," Peter said, "and there's a bounty on his head as we speak."

"So is that it?" Eloise asked, with a smile. "We can go home, back to good old Blighty?"

"Almost, my dear, almost. There's just a couple more things we need to do."

Peter reached into his pocket and drew out his calling card. The miniature cane. They watched as he unscrewed the top, dipped its silver nib in an inkwell and proceeded to write some notes on the hotel paper.

"Pens," he said. "Such a wonderful invention."

"Almost as good as time machines," Gerry said, laughing as he put his arm around Eloise.

"Let's go home, Els," he whispered.

"We were meant to be, Bumble," she whispered in return.

CHAPTER TWENTY-SIX

Monday 22nd October, 5.10 am

The robust uniformed sergeant who had not long arrived for duty, sat behind the desk with his feet up, sipping his regular morning coffee. He enjoyed the benefits of those early shifts; any bootlegging drunks would be snoring soundly in the cells, sleeping off a hangover and any self-respecting criminal would still be at home planning their crime. Not a lot happened at this hour of the day.

Finishing his coffee, he yawned with a stretch, leaning back in the chair, balancing it precariously on its two back legs to see how far he could go without toppling. He carefully pulled his truncheon from his holster and, reaching over, dragged an envelope that was sat on the desk towards his lap. Without seeing who it was addressed to, he prized it open and almost fell from the chair as he read the hand-written contents.

To whom it may concern

A bomb is somewhere in the Chicago Coliseum.'

CHAPTER TWENTY-SEVEN

Wednesday 31st October, Five Minutes to Midnight

The young man dressed in clothes unbefitting for such an occasion, moved his way through the throngs of tuxedos and ball gowns. Like a sparrow amidst a colony of penguins serenading peacocks, he made directly for the middle-aged, cigar smoking, man. The briefcase he carried by his side swung in time with the big band, as it played Nick Lucas's 'Someday, Somewhere'.

"Mr. Churchill?" he said, slipping his hand inside the case. "I've got something for you."

Winston Churchill looked up from the note he had been handed.

"What does it mean?" he shouted after the man. "Fight who on the beaches?"

But he was gone, lost in the crowd, smiling as he pulled the briefcase full of money to his chest. "The future," Clarence said.

CHAPTER TWENTY-EIGHT

Thursday 14th February, St Valentine's Day

The German Shepherd strained on its leash as it barked and howled, upset to be left tethered to the truck in one of Chicago's cold and oily North Side garages. His master, recently cut down in a hail of bullets, lay dead and unable to answer his cries.

"Shhh now, boy," the gun-wielding man said, as he straightened his policeman's jacket.

"Did we get him?" the second uniformed man asked.

"We gots him, alright," the first one replied. "He was the tall blonde one. German, I thinks."

Both men pointed their guns at their suited friends and together they walked from the garage, leaving seven bodies behind.

"Right lads. We best make this look real, so raise ya hands on the way out," the first man said.

Epilogue

"There's nothing," Gerry said, while studying the journal.

Eloise and Georgie sat in the two high-back leather chairs, watching as he paced the library. They had searched Kelsey Hall high and low since their return but found no sign of another secret room.

"I've read it cover to cover," Gerry continued, "but there is no key." He fanned the journal and even gave it a shake to prove his findings.

"Read that bit again, Bumble." Eloise said.

Gerry opened it to the page that held their only clue and once again recited the passage.

"The key's in the book,

And it's not so hard to find,

Just fill in the gap,

And you'll see that it's behind."

"Clarence was taking no chance of his device falling into the wrong hands, was he?" a voice behind them said. No-one had heard him enter the room. As per normal, Archie had seemed to appear from nowhere.

"Archie!" Eloise said. "Do you have any ideas? Did Granddad George tell you anything else?"

Archie walked over to join them and stood with his back to a wall of books that filled one end of the library.

"I'm afraid not, miss. It seems he and Clarence kept this one to themselves," he replied.

"Fill in the gap."

Georgie, who had been quiet up until that point, repeated his words.

"Fill in the gap," he said, smiling.

"Georgie?" Gerry said.

Georgie got up from his chair and joined Archie by the bookshelves.

"The key isn't in the book," he said, "It *is* the book."

"I don't understand," Eloise said, with a puzzled look on her face.

"Do you mind, old man?" he asked, taking the journal from Gerry. "It never occurred to me before and I thought nothing of it until this moment," he continued.

"What Daddy? What?" Eloise asked excitingly.

"Don't you remember, Els," he said "when you were a child, Grandmama and Grandpapa used to spend hours in this room?"

Eloise looked about the library, as if remembering her childhood days.

"Oh, Daddy! Yes, I do. Grandpapa always used to say that, one day, these books would be ours."

"That's right, Georgie interrupted, "and he also said it would fit into place in time."

"Yes, yes," Eloise laughed, "and I would run away giggling, shouting 'silly Grandpapa'."

Gerry, who had enjoyed seeing the look on Georgie and Eloise's faces as they reminisced, asked the next question.

"So, can I ask, where exactly is the key?"

"Right here," Georgie said, waving the journal in the air. "Let me show you. It wasn't until good old Archie came in and stood where he stands now that I saw it," he continued.

"Saw what, sir?" Archie asked, looking to his feet and up again.

"Strangely, Father always kept these books in order of subject and here, right between H.G Wells 'The Time Machine' and Samuel Madden's 'Memoirs of the Twentieth Century', one is missing."

"Of course," Gerry said. "Fill in the gap."

"Exactly. Shall I?" Georgie asked, as he held the journal before the empty space on the shelf.

One by one, they each gave their own reply.

"Yes, yes!" the still excited Eloise shrieked.

"It was meant to be, sir," Archie said.

Gerry simply nodded.

* * *

"Wow!" Gerry said, as they entered the large octagonal room hidden behind the library's false wall. "It seems someone's been busy."

"Indeed it does," Georgie replied, heading over to one of the book-filled walls.

Like the one before him, every wall was identical, filled floor to ceiling with leather-bound books, standing regimentally, as if they were soldiers on parade, the numbers embossed along the spines resembling the golden buttons of their tunics.

Tilting his head to one side, Georgie ran his finger along them, studying each one in turn.

"They're dated," he said.

Gerry turned on the spot, glancing at the abundance of books that surrounded them. Georgie was right; every book, on every shelf, was in chronological order, each depicting a calendar year.

Choosing one at random, Georgie slid it from the ranks and turned it over and over, examining it, looking for any other markings. There was nothing, just a plain green cover. No title or author, only the embossed date indicating the year 1585.

"That's strange," he said, opening the cover and leafing through the pages. "They're blank. Every page is blank."

"I wonder if this has something to do with it," Eloise asked.

Georgie ceased to leaf through the book and looked up at his daughter, who was now leaning over an octagonal metal table that sat dead centre in the room. Like the book, the table had no markings; its sides were smooth and ran parallel to the surrounding walls.

Gerry joined Eloise and studied their reflections in the slightly mirrored surface, which had a book-sized indentation set within.

"Georgie, could you find this year's book?" Gerry asked.

Joining him with the book labelled 1929, he handed it to Gerry, who placed it, spine down, into the slot. Almost immediately, it began to descend and all three watched as, inch by inch, it lowered, until finally it sat flush with the surface.

"Yep," Gerry thought, "just another ordinary day."

As if to confirm his thoughts, the table began to illuminate. Georgie and Eloise, not yet familiar with future technologies, instinctively backed away but Gerry watched in amazement, as neon lines started to appear and began connecting dates beneath the now opaque, azure blue surface. Headed by the words 'Gerry MacNeil', the lines were spread out across the table, forming what reminded Gerry of a family tree, each line joining significant events that had occurred since his arrival in 1928.

"What does that all mean?" Georgie questioned.

"By what I can make out," Gerry informed him, "it's my timeline."

"Your time what, old man?"

Gerry thought for a moment, studying the display before replying.

"It appears that this," indicating the tree-like diagram, "shows what has happened since I arrived here."

Georgie, who was now intrigued, stood at the table and pointed to the date 15/10/1928. As his finger touched the surface, the display changed to a step-by-step account of what Gerry had done at MI6 headquarters and the names of all those he had come into contact with, including the death of Miranda Love.

"Oh dear! Poor Miranda," Eloise said, as Georgie pulled his hand back sharply.

"Ah! I think I understand," Gerry said. "Now let's see what happens."

With a few swipes across the table, the display came to rest on that precise moment in time.

"There we go," he said.

"That's us!"

"Yes, Georgie look. April twenty first, 1929. Safe and sound."

A TIME FOR ADVENTURE

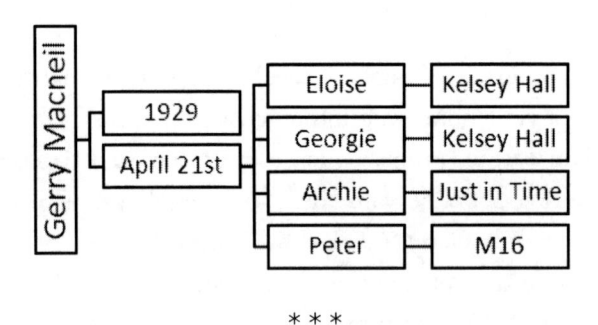

Gerry Macneil	1929 April 21st	Eloise	Kelsey Hall
		Georgie	Kelsey Hall
		Archie	Just in Time
		Peter	M16

* * *

Gerry held Eloise in his arms as they stood on the balcony overlooking the Scottish golf course, now bathed in warm sunlight.

The misty morning that Gerry had snuck along that very same balcony was now a memory but one that would be hard to forget.

"I promised myself I would bring you here, Els." he said, looking into her eyes.

"It's wonderful," she replied. "But?"

"But what, Els?"

Eloise's smile caught the sunlight as she replied.

"Where will our next adventure take us, I wonder?"

Acknowledgments

I thank my readers, present and future.

Special thanks go to
My editor Denise Watson.
For your great editing talents

Coming soon

Gerry MacNeil's next

Time Travel Adventure

It was dark, totally dark.

Gerry felt the weightlessness surrounding him, suffocating, yet strangely aerating with the sensation of spinning and falling in slow motion.

"Gerry?" a familiar female voice called from nowhere. From everywhere

"Bumble, where are you?"

Again the words echoed around him.

Opening his mouth to reply, his own words seemed to float silently before him, trapped in a bubble just like he remembered from the Beano or Dandy comics he would read as a kid.

He could see the letters E L O I S E, but they made no sound.

Also look out for

Escape and The Photographer

Other Titles by

Mel RJ Smith

Memoirs of an Ordinary Guy

Hoppy Lottie

https://authormelrjsmith.wordpress.com/

Twitter @melrjsmith